"Alexa Riley delivers a feel-good romance with addictive helpings of secrets, suspense, and revenge!"
—*The Rock Stars of Romance* on *Everything for Her*

"Alexa Riley has given me everything I want and more. Sizzling passion, a devoted and loyal hero and a safe love story that has me sighing with pleasure at the end."
—Nichole, *Sizzling Pages*, on *Everything for Her*

"It's what Alexa Riley fantasies are made of—Sugar and Spice and Everything Kinky and Nice!"
—Yaya, *After Dark Book Lovers*, on *Everything for Her*

"Full of big attitude and intense chemistry, I had lots of fun watching these two deal with their feelings and in Paige's case, finally letting someone into her heart."
—*Harlequin Junkie* on *His Alone*

"A great addition to the series that is still growing."
—*Night Owl Reviews* on *Stay Close*

"The AR recipe in full force: virgin, claiming, instant love, fast marriage, babies. If it ain't broke…"
—*The Book Disciple* on *Hold Tight*

Also available from Alexa Riley and Carina Press

For Her

Everything for Her
His Alone
Claimed

For You

Stay Close
Hold Tight
Don't Go

FOR YOU COMPLETE COLLECTION

STAY CLOSE
HOLD TIGHT
DON'T GO

ALEXA RILEY

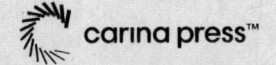

carina press™

If you purchased this book without a cover you should be aware that this book is stolen property. It was reported as "unsold and destroyed" to the publisher, and neither the author nor the publisher has received any payment for this "stripped book."

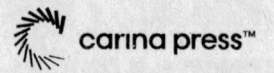

carina press™

ISBN-13: 978-1-335-00811-4

For You Complete Collection

This edition copyright © 2018 by Author Alexa Riley LLC

The publisher acknowledges the copyright holder of the individual works as follows:

Stay Close
Copyright © 2017 by Author Alexa Riley LLC

Hold Tight
Copyright © 2017 by Author Alexa Riley LLC

Don't Go
Copyright © 2018 by Author Alexa Riley LLC

All rights reserved. Except for use in any review, the reproduction or utilization of this work in whole or in part in any form by any electronic, mechanical or other means, now known or hereafter invented, including xerography, photocopying and recording, or in any information storage or retrieval system, is forbidden without the written permission of the publisher, Harlequin Enterprises Limited, 22 Adelaide St. West, 40th Floor, Toronto, Ontario M5H 4E3, Canada.

This is a work of fiction. Names, characters, places and incidents are either the product of the author's imagination or are used fictitiously, and any resemblance to actual persons, living or dead, business establishments, events or locales is entirely coincidental.

This edition published by arrangement with Harlequin Books S.A.

® and TM are trademarks of the publisher. Trademarks indicated with ® are registered in the United States Patent and Trademark Office, the Canadian Intellectual Property Office and in other countries.

www.CarinaPress.com

Printed in U.S.A.

Recycling programs for this product may not exist in your area.

CONTENTS

STAY CLOSE	7
HOLD TIGHT	101
DON'T GO	187

STAY CLOSE

For Daisy... We miss you every day.

Prologue

Ivan

She loves to dance.

Her small body moves with the dark beat of the bass as I throw back a shot of vodka. There is no burn when the liquid warmth hits my tongue and melts down my throat. I clench the glass because I can't put my hands where I want them.

The seductive curve of her waist as it cascades to the flare of her hips... I watch transfixed when they move side to side. Side to side. Her body is like the pendulum inside a grandfather clock, and I can't look away.

The music is deafening, but if she were to simply whisper my name, I would be at her feet, begging to touch what I shouldn't, taste what doesn't belong to me, run my hands along the sweet innocence she taunts me with. An innocence I shouldn't want but crave. Something so pure and untouched like nothing I've ever known before.

Slamming the glass down on the bar, I'm both disappointed and relieved when it doesn't break. Maybe the cut of the glass could cool the feelings I have pulsing though me but I doubt it. Not with her. I'm not sure anything ever could. I would welcome a pain that's greater than my ache for her. For there is nothing more powerful than the spell she has me under.

I've been hired to protect her.

But as I push away from the bar and walk towards her, I can't help but think that perhaps someone should have protected her from me.

Chapter One

Penelope

I lean up against the wall in the hallway, trying to determine what's being said inside my mom and dad's office. I've been standing out here for over twenty minutes and can't make out a word. In fact, I'm not even sure they're speaking English. I saw the man who came to have a meeting with them shortly after dinner. It was odd because my parents never bring their work home. The moment my eyes met his, something funny happened inside me. He stole the breath right out of my lungs, something no boy had ever done before.

It might have to do with the fact that he was far from a boy. That beast was all man, maybe even something more. A man who looked like he could kill someone with the flick of his wrist. And the weirdest part—how could someone who looked so menacing draw me in? Call to something deep inside me. Something that I didn't even know was there until I saw him.

My parents run the entire security and protection division for one of the top companies in the world, so

I've been around a lot of people who look deadly. My sister and I have whispered that we think at one time our father worked undercover for the government. At least that's what Pandora, my twin, thinks. I believe her, because Pandora notices everything. You can't get much past her.

This guy seems dark and deadly, from his eyes that are so brown they're almost black, to his jet-black hair that's been buzzed short. It looks like he doesn't have the time—or the inclination—to do anything with it. The way he walked in and how he held himself makes me think he doesn't give much thought to how he looks. Someone like him doesn't care what others think, and that kind of confidence is sexy. It's different than what I'm used to with the boys at school. That difference draws me to him.

I caught sight of tattoos that ran along his knuckles and hands before disappearing under his coat. Then they peeked out again, up around the collar of his jacket, making me think that most of his big body was covered in ink. And the man was big.

He wasn't like most of the men who work for my dad. They look like they could take you in a fight, but they're always clean-cut and in suits. Not this man. I don't know what it was about him, but I was drawn to him instantly.

He isn't my normal type, not that I really have a type at all. I'm only eighteen, so I'm not sure I've decided that yet. The boys I talk to at school would fall under the preppy category, but that's pretty much every guy there. It's private and caters to kids with some of the richest parents in New York City. No one there is running around with tattoos covering their body.

"Not this one, Penny."

I jump a little at my sister's soft words. She's standing next to me with her back against the wall as well, as if she's been there the whole time.

"How do you do that?" I whisper at her. Jesus. Everyone in this freaking house is like a spy or something. They move around like cats, never making a noise. When I move, people don't normally miss me coming. I'm loud and pretty clumsy.

She shoots me a smirk, and I roll my eyes. She reaches out her hand and links it with mine. "You weren't in bed."

"Because I'm spying," I whisper a little too loudly and cringe at myself.

I'm sure I'm doing a terrible job at sneaking around. You'd think living with Pandora and my parents, I would have picked up some tricks. But I should have known my sister would catch me. We're twins and have had our own rooms since we turned thirteen, but she still ends up in my bed most nights. She doesn't sleep well when she's alone. I like it, though. Pandora has always been the strong one, even when we were growing up. She gives no shits, whereas I'm the girly girl who gets her feelings hurt about everything. But at the end of the day, Pandora is still the one crawling into my bed. It makes me feel like I also have a way of making her feel safe. Just like she always did with me growing up. From school playgrounds to asshole boys, Pandora was always there to put someone in their place.

"They probably know you're out here," she whispers back, and I shrug.

I don't care. I want another look at the dark stranger. Something about him has piqued my curiosity, and I feel drawn to him. Maybe it's the mystery, or maybe it's that he seems like a challenge. It could be that while I find the darkness in his eyes sexy, they still seem a little lonely. My weakness is seeing someone else hurting, and I caught a glimpse of that. It calls to me.

"Not him, Penny. Stick to the boys at school."

I look over at her. We look exactly the same, but I have my father's green eyes and Pandora has our mother's deep blue eyes. We're both built like her, though. We're both petite with small features and deep red hair. Our eyes are really the only way to tell us apart. That is, until one of us opens our mouth. Then it's easy to tell who's who.

I feel warmth hit my cheeks. I'm not shocked she knew I was standing out here trying to get another look at him, but I'm still a little embarrassed. I've always been a little boy crazy, but it never lasts long. I crush for a second and then jump on to the next. For some reason, when I know they like me back, I lose interest fast. Pandora always jokes that I'm in love with having a crush, and once the crush is gone, so am I.

"Something feels off. I can't put my finger on it, but he's rough around the edges. You need someone sweet."

She's right. Something does feel different with him, but it's a kind of different I don't want to stay away from. As crazy as it sounds I think he's mine. I don't know why but when I saw him, it was all I could think.

"Fuck," she mumbles, probably reading my face.

The door to our parents' office opens, making us both jump away from the wall. Our mom stands in the doorway, her hands on her hips. "What are you two doing?"

"I wanted to see if we could stay late after school tomorrow to study for finals," Pandora says quickly.

She's fast on her toes to cover up for us. She's always been that way, even when we were little. I would get a bright idea, like covering our room in sparkles, and she'd tell me not to. Then I would do it anyway, because, well, I have terrible impulse control, and when we'd get busted she'd always say it was her idea. Always my protector.

She squeezes my hand, still locked in hers.

Mom rolls her eyes, clearly not believing her. My gaze goes to the shadow behind her. He's looking right at me. My heart jumps into my throat. I can't look away from him. Pandora gives my hand another hard squeeze, silently telling me to stop staring. Finally I drop my eyes from his, instantly missing the connection.

"Fine. Your dad and I have a meeting tomorrow and will be working late. Your security will be waiting outside the school for the both of you."

"I want to go for a run after," I tell her.

I've been stuck with Pandora and her security guard since I ditched my last one. Dad made me stick with Pandora's security and got rid of mine for losing me the last time. I should have felt bad, but the guy totally gave me the creeps. He'd always find ways to touch me, and the touches started to linger a little too long.

I love my family, but all of them want to keep me in

Bubble Wrap. They aren't even like this with Pandora. Everyone thinks I'm the soft one, which is probably true. I'm not into self-defense, and I really don't care about anything pertaining to safety and security. I'm into cooking, dressing up, dancing and singing at the top of my lungs. And probably boys. But after today, I'm crossing boys off that list. Men. One man in particular is climbing to the top of that list.

"Well, you're in luck. We found you a new bodyguard." My mom glances over her shoulder at my new obsession, and my heart rate spikes. I could not be this lucky. I glance over and see his eyes are still on me, but I can't read his face with so little light. "Penelope, this is Ivan. I don't think you'll be able to lose this one."

My mom smirks, and I have to bite my lip to keep from smiling. Ivan is most definitely a man I won't try to run from.

I hear Pandora mumble "*fuck*" under her breath as his dark eyes narrow on me.

Chapter Two

Ivan

I tighten the laces on my shoes and then tuck my knife into the strap at my ankle. I cover it up with the leg of my slacks and then walk over to the closet to grab a shirt.

I've moved into the guest house at the Justices', although it would be hard to consider this anything but a mansion. There are two other personal bodyguards covering the family, but they maintain residence elsewhere and only stay the night out here when necessary.

The guest quarters are within walking distance to the main house but still offer some privacy. Originally I didn't want to move onto the property, but Paige said I owed her. Which is true.

I was raised in Renza, Russia, just outside Moscow. I did labor on the railways there as a young boy until one of the older guys came around one day looking for runners. I didn't know at the time what that meant, but he offered up money, and I knew exactly what that was.

My mother died during childbirth, and no one knew

who my father was, so I was given to an orphanage. I ran away when I was ten and found work where I could. The place I ran from wasn't looking to chase down another mouth to feed, so I became a child of the street and did what I could to survive.

I started off taking packages after I finished the rail work for the day, but eventually I was trusted with more deliveries. The money was far more than I could make doing an honest day's work, and back then I needed to eat. It was all about surviving. I was loyal to those who treated me with even half an ounce of decency, but as time went on, I began to harden my heart. Lines started to cross and I started to lose myself.

Years went on, and I became a part of the Russian underground mafia. The organization was dirty, and as much as I wanted to be loyal, I couldn't do some of the things they asked me to. I didn't have another life beyond this makeshift family, and I did what I could to survive.

But as with all men, power and greed began to take over, and the underground changed hands. Dissent simmered in the ranks, and everyone was trying to get off the sinking ship before they got pulled back in. I knew I didn't want to go down, like I said, everything was about surviving, and members were being killed off one by one. There was nothing in that life worth dying for. I knew I had to get out and did what I had to.

The one thing I did have was information, and it was useful. I got a coded message sent to me at the perfect time, and I was ready for it. The contact wanted information on a deal that was taking place between a corporate giant in America and a country in southern Asia. They were concerned it could have potential ties to the Russian mafia and they wanted the Asian company vetted.

I agreed to turn over what I had in exchange for safe passage out of Russia. I wanted to disappear, and this was the perfect opportunity. I could leave my homeland and have a simple life somewhere far away. I never had dreams of fortune or fame. I was only ever just a boy trying to survive the winter. My choices led me down a dark path, one that at first I had no choice but to take, and I was ready to start over.

I found out my name was on a shortlist of those being terminated from the original underground, so I made my move. My death was staged in an explosion of a warehouse that I was living in at the time. The scene was made to look like I'd been taken out by someone looking to make a name for himself in the ranks. I found out later that the person who claimed responsibility was someone I trusted. He was killed two days later.

I arrived in Italy a week after with nothing but the clothes on my back and a USB drive in my pocket. My contact at Osbourne Corporation had been true to their word and gotten me across the borders.

Jordan Chen was waiting for me at a café by the sea in Genoa. I gave him all the information I had and then some. He gave me a new name and passport, but then he gave me something else.

"What's this?"

"An opportunity," Jordan says, packing up his stuff.

"So I go from one master to another?" I ask angrily.

"No. You don't owe us anything. After I walk away we're done here." There is honesty in his eyes, which is a contrast to the scar on his face. *"If you're interested, we could use someone like you on this side of the world. It doesn't have to be you, but you're our first choice. Plus, the pay is enough for you to retire in a year or two."*

I hadn't given much thought to what I was going to do next. My biggest hurdle was getting out of the country undetected.

"Think it over. When you've made your decision, call the number."

I look down at the card that's on top of the stack of papers. The name Paige Justice is embossed in gold, and her number is below. I'm not prepared to become someone else's watchdog, but I don't know if I can say no.

So that's what I've done the past five years. I've worked for Osbourne Corp International, vetting companies they're either interested in taking over or want to do business with. I've spent my time following businessmen and digging into their lives. It's easy work and a lot more legal than I ever was with the mafia. But just like before, it's a lonely world, and I'm tired of the isolation. Something was missing and I wasn't sure I knew what it was. How can someone feel lonely or understand what it really is if it's all they really ever had? But I felt it. I craved something else. Deep down to my bones I knew I was looking for something or someone.

Last month I sent Paige a message telling her I wanted out. She said her husband Ryan had a replacement whenever I was ready to go. I was both relieved and disappointed she didn't ask me to stay on. Although I knew I wanted a life of my own, I liked being needed. Even if it was a business on the other side of the world.

To my surprise, I got a message the next day from Paige saying that I owed her one last favor and asking me to come to the States.

I'd met both Ryan and Paige several times over the years. They'd come to Europe on vacation and we'd end up talking business for hours. I respected the two of them and thought that they worked well together as a team. There were also times I'd become jealous, seeing the love they shared, and had to excuse myself. It was difficult to be around two people who adored one another so much, knowing that I'd never find that kind of love myself. A woman who wanted me, who was soft and sweet. All I ever seemed to draw in were women who wanted darkness. Who thought I would be rough. It would make my stomach roll at the thought of something like that. I wanted the sweetness I saw between them. The love and devotion. Not the pain and darkness.

I decided that I'd repay the debt and go to America. And when I arrived, they told me that they'd like me to protect one of their daughters. Something that sounded simple enough.

I finish getting dressed and make my way through the garden that separates the guest quarters from the main house. I agreed to stay here for a trial period until we figure out something more permanent. Penelope is still deciding on colleges, they said, and they don't want to make any decision yet.

When I get to the back of the house, I catch a glimpse of her at the table from my position at the glass doors outside the kitchen.

As if I've spoken her name aloud, she turns to face me, and our eyes lock. Her green eyes are like nothing I've seen before. A sweet, pure innocence pours off her in waves, touching me deep in my soul in a place I didn't even know was there.

My chest fills with warmth as a chill runs from the back of my neck down my spine. It's exactly like last night all over again.

I've never felt more powerless with one look.

Chapter Three

Penelope

"Penny!" The loud whisper from my sister has me opening one eye to look at her.

"What?" I moan, pulling the pillow over my head.

I debate whether to use the same trick my parents did with us when they went from a king-size bed to a full so we couldn't sleep with them anymore. Though I would have to get a twin to get Pandora out of mine.

"I'm hungry." Her words come out in a pout. I don't even have to see her face to know the expression she's making right now.

"And the sky is blue." I roll over and pull the pillow off my head, looking at my alarm clock. The damn thing hasn't even gone off yet. She's always hungry. "What the flip, Pan? It's not even time to get up." I throw the pillow at her. She catches it easily and tosses it back on the bed.

"I gotta go in early. Forgot to finish up my paper for art history, and I need those stupid books in the library."

This isn't shocking. Pandora hates homework. If she

could skate by on tests she would be golden. This year we didn't get any of the same classes, so she doesn't have me reminding her about what's due anymore.

"What do you want?" I ask, pulling myself from the bed.

"Bacon and pancakes," I hear her say from behind me. "Oh, and scrambled eggs with—"

"I know how you like your eggs," I tell her, cutting her off. I've been making this family breakfast almost every morning since I was old enough to be in the kitchen alone.

"You rock!" she yells, running from my room to get ready.

I make my way to the kitchen and start breakfast, and I work on packing everyone's lunch at the same time. Today I make tomato turkey sandwiches with a sweet glaze on slices of fresh bread.

"Sweetheart," my dad greets me, coming into the kitchen and placing a kiss on top of my head.

"Hey, Dad. Bacon and pancakes today," I tell him, handing him a plate.

He gives me another kiss on the head before sitting down at the breakfast bar and digging in. My mom walks in the kitchen a few minutes later, and my dad is on his feet, pulling her chair out for her then giving her a deep kiss. I roll my eyes but smile as I go back to packing everyone lunches.

My parents can be a little too PDA for me at times, but I wouldn't want them any other way. My dad and mom were made for each other, and I hope one day I find that, too. An image of Ivan from the night before flutters through my mind, as do some of the dreams I'd had about him. My cheeks start to heat as I remember them, particularly the one of him kissing me over and over again. And the one where I trace his tattoos, though the images of that one are fuzzy, which means I might need to get a better look at them.

I'm thankful I'm not facing my parents so they can't see the blush lighting up my face.

"Lock it up."

I jump, not realizing Pandora walked into the room. She's eating a piece of bacon while her eyes narrow on me.

"Don't you have somewhere to be?" I glare back at her, handing her a to-go plate she can eat in the car on her way to school.

"I'm watching you," she mouths, and I have to bite back my retort: *So what's new?* She takes the plate from me before going over to my parents and telling them goodbye. She throws her hand up in a wave on the way out.

"Did she forget to finish something?" my mom asks me, and I nod.

Dad chuckles. They can't really get mad at her. She might not like school, but she's always pulled straight A's. We both do, even at one of the toughest private schools in the country.

Since we're both great in school and don't give them too much grief, our parents are pretty good about giving us free rein as long as we keep a guard with us. Rules loosened up a lot since we turned eighteen. And then when Pandora punched Ethan, a boy at prom who tried to kiss me, that gained us some more freedom. I cringe at the memory.

I bet Ivan could take a punch and not even care. He doesn't seem like he would run scared after like Ethan did. He was a nice enough boy, but I wasn't ready for how handsy he was getting, and Pandora knew right away. Then I start to wonder what it would be like if it were Ivan making the same moves...

"We'll be a little late tonight, honey," Mom says, shaking me out of my fantasy. She comes around and puts her dish in the sink. "Thank you for breakfast."

"Will you be home in time for dinner?"

"Don't you have finals to study for?" she asks as my dad comes to stand behind her. He wraps an arm around her, and she melts into him.

"Yeah, but cooking always helps me relax," I remind her. I know they always feel a little guilty that I cook for everyone, but I love it. It's one of my favorite things to do. That's why Pandora knew I would get out of bed this morning to make her something to eat.

"You know I can't turn down your cooking." Mom leans in and gives me another kiss. "Do me a favor, Penelope, and don't be hard on the new guy." She levels me with a stare.

"Who, me?" I bat my lashes, which makes my dad laugh.

"I wonder where she got this thing for ditching her guards," Dad says right before Mom elbows him. My dad fakes like he's hurt. "You're going to kiss that later."

"Okay, you two need to go to work," I say, handing them their lunches. I don't want to hear their flirting.

Dad gives me a hug and another kiss on the head before leaving the kitchen. I smile as they depart, and then I turn around to make my own plate.

I grab my phone and start up some music on it. After I find a song I like, I start dancing a little as I take a few bites of my food. I look around the kitchen to make sure I have stuff to make tacos for dinner tonight, wondering when Ivan will get here. As soon as the thought pops into my head, I turn around and freeze when I see him standing in the backyard, staring at me.

My breath catches as our eyes meet. Today he's in black slacks and a buttoned-up white collared shirt. The sleeves are rolled up, and I can see a bit more of his tattoos today. There's still so much of him that's hidden, but I think that's part of the attraction.

I can't pull my eyes from him as he starts to move towards me. I'm rooted in place as his long, thick legs eat up the distance between us. He stops at the glass doors that line the far wall of our kitchen, then he slides the door open and lets himself right in.

I lick my lips as he closes it and leans up against it. His eyes never leave mine, and he doesn't utter a word. I don't know how long we stand there until I'm finally able to pull enough air into my lungs to say something.

"Hungry?" I nod to the food that's sitting on the kitchen counter. It's not normal for us to have leftovers, but everyone seemed to be in a hurry this morning, so there's plenty for him.

"You'd feed me?" Ivan asks, his dark eyebrows pulling together as if he's confused. It's then I hear an accent that I think is Russian. His voice is seriously deep. Deeper than any voice I've ever heard before.

"It's kinda my thing. I feed people around here," I tease, finding a little more of my voice again. Jesus, what is wrong with me? I'm never tongue-tied when I'm around guys, but Ivan is different. He's head to toe man, and this instant attraction is something I've never experienced before.

He steps farther into the room, so I grab a plate and serve him some of the food. When I turn around he's standing right behind me. I have to look up at him. His inscrutable dark eyes are locked on me.

"Sorry, there's only one piece of bacon left. I'm shocked there's even that," I say, a little more breathily than I mean to.

I feel a tug on the plate, and I let go, knowing he grabbed it. I don't look down to see because our eyes remain locked.

"I would eat anything you served me," he says simply, and I feel myself blush.

The thought of other things he could eat enters my mind, and I have to turn around. I don't want to get caught thinking of such a dirty image, because I feel like he can read it all over my face. Oh. My. God. Something is wrong with me.

I start cleaning up the kitchen, trying to distract myself with something, anything. As I grab a plate in the sink, he reaches out, taking it from my hand.

"You cooked for me, I will clean for you."

I should probably tell him that we have someone who comes in and does this for us. I was only doing it because I was trying to stay busy in an effort to not make a fool of myself.

"Perhaps you should get dressed."

His eyes travel down my body, and embarrassment floods me. It's then I realize I'm in sleep shorts that are more like underwear and a Harry Potter shirt that says *I'm up to no good*. It's so faded it's almost see-through. At one time it belonged to my mom, but I love it so much because I remember her reading the books to Pandora and me when we were little. She wore it all the time until I stole it about five years ago.

"Okay," I whisper, and then I actually do something my guard told me to do. I turn to leave, but he grabs my wrist. I stop short and stand there, with him holding on to me. I look into his dark eyes, and I'm unable to move. There's so much there that I can't read, but I recognize one thing for sure.

"Are you up to no good, *krasota*?" The low words rumble from his chest, and they vibrate through me.

I lick my lips, wondering what that word means. I'm surprised by his question. There's an edge of danger in it, and it doesn't feel like he's only asking as a concerned guard looking out for me.

"I guess you'll have to find out for yourself," I whisper before pulling my arm from him and leaving the room.

I feel his eyes on my back the whole time, and I remember what I saw there. It was like nothing I'd ever seen before, and I want it again. No man has ever looked at me like that before.

With pure desire.

Chapter Four

Ivan

This was a mistake.

I can feel the burn of my palm where I touched her soft skin. The way I reached out and grabbed her was unlike me. I try not to touch people if possible, and there I was, holding on to her delicate wrist and trying to make her stay. She's having an effect on me like nothing I've experienced, and I don't know if I can handle it but I want it like nothing I've ever wanted before.

She sits beside me silently as I drive her to school. It's only the two of us, and the space feels somehow intimate. I want to hear her talk again. Her voice does something to me. It's like a balm on my soul. I don't care if she just reads the dictionary. I want to hear her voice.

"How do you know my parents? I've never seen you before."

The question breaks the peace slinging though me, and though I have a need to not lie to her, I don't know how much of the truth I'm willing to tell her. I pause for a moment to think of a way to phrase my answer, but she takes this to mean that I won't answer.

"Fine. Forget I asked." She looks out the window, and I can see hurt in her reflection on the glass.

"*Net*. No." I hurriedly switch from Russian to English. "I'm trying to think of a way to tell you without revealing what is confidential," I admit, only wanting to give her the truth. Lying to such a pure soul seems wrong.

"Oh," she says, turning to look at me. "You don't have to if you can't. I was just curious. You're different to all their other...choices."

I think about the other guards she's been around, and I tighten my grip on the steering wheel. I don't like the thought of her being seen so much, and by men who could overpower her. Maybe I should look into the past men. I don't see how they could have let her out of their sight so easily.

"I helped them with overseas contracts. I was an informant," I finally tell her.

"And you're not anymore?" she asks.

"I'm here to protect you." Something about those words makes pride fill my chest. As if this is the job I've been training my whole life for. I've run with dirty criminals to learn how to read them. I've been made into a weapon to protect this perfect creature I'm sure everyone wants, and only I can keep them all at bay. It's my life's goal and I will not fail in this. She needs my protection. She needs me. Even if it's a lie, the thought fills me with pride, my past not seeming so dirty because I've been training for this. For her.

She's quiet for a moment, and then I feel her eyes on me as I stare ahead at the road. "What word did you call me in the kitchen?"

I want to curse myself for the slip, but I cannot deny her what she asks for. "Beauty."

There is another long pause at this admission, and I don't know if she is offended by this or welcomes it.

"What can I call you?" Her voice is quiet, but I hear the smile in it, and my heart brightens at the thought.

"Ivan," I say, looking over and seeing the brightness of her green eyes.

"No, I mean like a nickname." She thinks for a second. "What do your friends call you?"

"I don't have friends," I answer honestly.

She rolls her eyes and hits my arm playfully. "Okay, I'll be your friend. Jeez. Stop begging." When I smile at her, a little shade of pink rises in her cheeks, and it is so lovely. The most perfect thing I have ever seen. I never knew pink could be so beautiful. "All right, friend. What can I call you for a nickname?"

"Is Ivan not sufficient?"

She taps her finger on her chin as if she's thinking it over. "What about something in Russian?"

The thought of her trying to speak the language is both comical and enticing. I would love to have her under me in the dark and whisper words of seduction to her in my mother tongue. I have to stop myself from following down that path of thoughts or it could lead to trouble.

"Maybe once you think of something, I could teach you the words." It's the best compromise I can offer.

"I'd like that." She looks out the window and points to a space. "You can park there. I can walk from here."

"I will escort you, *krasota*. Please sit, and I will help you exit the car." She looks away from me, but I see the smile pulling at her lips before she does it.

I park and then walk around the car to open her door and hold my hand out for her to take it. I feel the softness of her palm but also the heated beat of her heart. It matches my own, and something about that makes me possessive of her.

She steps out, and though I am reluctant to let go of her hand, I do. I grab her bag and hold it for her as we walk onto the school campus. Large iron fencing marks the perimeter, and a courtyard sits just beyond it.

"Okay, if you come in any farther, it's going to look like I've got a babysitter instead of a friend." She smiles at me, and there is kindness in her eyes. "I'll be at that bench for lunch, if you want to join me."

She points to a space under a maple tree, and I nod.

"No pressure. Some of my guards didn't wait all day, but some of them did. Either way, I'll see you right here at three."

"Have a pleasant day, Penelope," I say, and she laughs a little. I love the sound and want to hear it again. "Did I not say that right?"

"You did. It was just kind of cute. Your English is really good, it's just a little bit proper."

I nod, not wanting to embarrass myself again.

I hold out her bag, and she takes it from me. Our hands brush, and for a moment we stand there, silent. The feel of her delicate skin against my rough, tattooed hand is unlike anything I've experienced. She's innocent and pure, and I'm nothing like that. The thought should make me pull away, but instead I run my index finger along the inside of her wrist and watch as her pupils dilate. The black takes over the deep green and I can see the want in her eyes. I'm affecting her just as her presence is pushing down all of my walls.

Taking a step back, I break the connection and try to do what I know is right. I should keep my distance and then explain to Paige that I can't do this job anymore. That I'm compromised in some way and can't be trusted. But the thought of her with someone else this close to her rips my heart in half. She is mine. I feel it deep down in a place I didn't even know was there.

So even though I know I'm not good enough for her, I can't allow her to slip from my grasp. I want something good in my life. That could be her. That will be her. I try and reassure myself so I can let her go.

She walks away from me, and the distance that's growing is maddening. I want to walk after her and have her talk to me more, have her ask me questions and tell me her most precious secrets. Instead of chasing after her I walk back to the car and wait.

Glancing at my watch I see that I have four hours until I can be by her side again. The wait is going to be agonizing, but I will do it. Because even a second in her presence is worth hours alone.

Nothing good can come from my growing obsession. Yet I know I will do nothing to stop it.

Chapter Five

Penelope

I can't seem to sit still as I fidget with the book I got from the school library. I'm not paying any attention to what my economics teacher is saying. I want to open the book and look through it, but I know Mrs. Smarten will scold me if I do. She'll probably make me go to the whiteboard to answer questions she thinks I missed. God, I can't wait to be out of high school already, though I know what will come next. I push the thoughts of college out of my mind. The large stack of acceptance letters are waiting to be dealt with, but I don't want to think about it right now. At this moment, school isn't anywhere on my radar.

I glance over at the clock for the tenth time in the past two minutes. I don't think I've ever been this excited for lunch, and I love food. That's got to mean something. But I'm not concerned with eating. I only want to see him again. I want to sit next to him and see how he responds to me. He's so different than anyone I've ever met before.

I bite my lip to keep from smiling as I think about his little nickname for me. Then I wonder if it's a Russian term that everyone uses. Kind of like we use "honey" or "sweetheart" in America. Maybe he uses it with a lot of people. Then again, I can't see Ivan walking around calling things beautiful. I want the name to be mine and no one else's.

He broke a piece of my heart when he said he didn't have any friends. Is it because he's new to America? I tried to lighten the mood by making a joke, but I actually don't think that he cared that he didn't have any. It was as if it was normal for him to be alone. I didn't ask him if he had family. Or a wife. Crap.

What if he isn't out there when I go to lunch? He didn't answer when I told him where I'd be. The thought of him not showing up makes an emptiness take hold inside me. In all the time we've had guards on us, I've never liked it. Always being watched, always having eyes on me was annoying. I knew it made my parents relax a little and they weren't so uptight when we had our detail, but I still had moments of rebellion against it.

My parents run the security and protection division at Osbourne Corporation. It's my uncle Miles's business, but I'm not sure what they do. Something about investments and buying things. Whatever it is, he's made a lot of international purchases, and that can sometimes make people angry. My mom and dad might be overly cautious, but they think it's better to be safe. We're all family, which means any of us could be a target. That includes Pandora and our cousin, Henry. No one ever goes into details about why they are so protective, but I think there must be a story behind it.

As much as I hated my guards, I knew they were a necessity. Even when I was busy trying to give them the slip, I wasn't being reckless. Most of the time I just went home. But the thought of running from Ivan is almost ridiculous. In fact, here I sit, hoping he will be there when I go outside to have my lunch. I like his eyes on me. They look at me with heated curiosity, as if he isn't sure what to do with me.

When the teacher finally dismisses us I almost trip over my own feet trying to get out of the classroom as quick as possible. When I hit the hallway I see Pandora standing like she's waiting for me. She likely wants to have lunch together, something we do a few times a week. The other times she spends it in the library doing her homework so she doesn't have to do it when she gets home.

"Hey," I say, trying to play it cool, but she shakes her head and her ponytail bounces back and forth. At school it's easier for people to tell us apart. We have to wear uniforms, and girls have the option of slacks or a skirt. I wear a skirt, but Pandora always wears slacks. She plays down her looks whereas I've always been the one to dress up. I almost cried the day I could finally fit into our mom's shoes. I could shamelessly do a wardrobe change four times a day.

"New guy bring you to school today?"

"Yep" is all I give her. Because she knew the answer to the question before she even asked. Pandora and I both have had our driver's licenses since we were sixteen, but our parents still insist on us being driven around.

"Where we eating?" she asks.

"I'm guessing you're eating in the library to finish your art history paper." I have a feeling she still isn't done with it. She could have put it off until the last second, but Pandora can be a perfectionist, too. So whatever she did this morning, she'll still want to go over.

She growls in the same way Mom does when Dad makes her mad.

"I'm still watching you," she warns, putting two fingers to her eyes and then pointing them back and forth between us. I roll my eyes.

"Watch my backside." I wink at her before turning around and moving towards where I hope Ivan will be.

"Penny, I'm serious with this one. He's not a boy you can toy with like here at school."

I turn around and glare at her because people likely heard her in the hallway. "Love you, Pan, but I'm eighteen. You're not always going to be around to watch my every step."

"I love you, too," is all she says, shaking her head and walking away.

I know her words were more than love and affection. They're also a reminder that she does what she does *because* she loves me. I feel the same, but I have to be able to break away and make my own choices. I can't stay in the Bubble Wrap they want to keep me in forever.

Pulling my phone out of my bag, I see I have a text from my dad telling me to have a great day, followed by a bunch of emojis. I smile down at my phone and send one back.

I stop when I run into a wall. Not a wall, actually, just a very big man. My eyes travel up to Ivan's face. His hands are locked on my shoulders, keeping me from falling on my ass. I smile even bigger now that he's here.

"Hi," I say, and try to move in a little closer to him. His dark eyes travel down my face to the phone in my hand.

"What was making you smile," he finally says, nodding towards the phone. "Was it a boyfriend?" he asks as his eyes narrow. Then he begins to glance around us. "Does he go here?" That question sounds like a threat, like if there were a boyfriend, he'd take care of it.

My smile widens further. I like his jealousy so much more than I should. Now I know what it means. He likes me. I can tell from the spark in his eyes that his comment isn't about protecting me.

"I'm smiling now because you came to have lunch with me." He fixes his gaze on me again, no longer looking for my nonexistent boyfriend. "Before, it was my dad. He likes to send goofy messages to Pandora and me throughout the day."

The lines around his mouth ease, and I see tension leave his body. He nods then reaches out, taking my bag from off my shoulder and my phone from my hand.

"Your lunch break isn't long, and you must eat." He looks over to the bench I'd told him about, and I slip my arm into his.

His body freezes for a moment, and he stares down at me, surprise on his face.

"No boyfriend," I tell him. "Do you have a girlfriend? A wife?" I swear I stop breathing at my question.

"*Net*."

I feel myself relax. I notice my reaction is the same one he had when I told him I didn't have a boyfriend.

"I find that hard to believe," I tease him, pulling him over towards the bench and sitting down. I take my bag from him.

"It is not hard to believe. I've never had a girlfriend or a wife."

I still at his words, then drag my eyes from him and dig in my bag for my lunch. "Do you have a family, Ivan?"

"*Net*," he says easily as he inputs the code to unlock my phone. I would ask how he knows the code, but I don't. With a family that works in security, I know nothing is really private. But I don't care about my phone right now. I'm still ruminating on the ease with which he told me he doesn't have a family. No emotion crossed his face when he made that confession.

"I don't have your number," I tell him, finally getting him to look away from my phone. "What if I need you and I can't get a hold of you."

"I will never be far enough away from you that you could yell my name and I wouldn't hear you."

"But what if I want to say something to you that I don't want anyone to hear." I slide a little closer to him. He looks back down at the phone, and I watch him program his number in.

"You can call me anytime you like," he says, handing me my phone back. I slide it into my bag, and I open up my lunch.

"Do you track me on the phone?" I ask.

I don't know why I ask, because I already know the answer. But for some reason I want to hear him say he does. I think I'm losing it. Something that drove me crazy days ago is now something I want.

"*Da*," he confirms, but he doesn't seem to like his own answer. "I do not like cell phone tracking. I don't think it works as well as others."

I open my sandwich and try to hand him half, but he shakes his head.

"But I made it. Didn't you like your breakfast?"

"It was the most wonderful meal I've ever eaten. But I will not eat your lunch. You need to eat it."

I love his sweet answer and even feel myself blush a little that he liked my cooking. "Please. Just half a sandwich." I give him the little pout that works on my family, and watch his eyes go wide for a second.

"If it pleases you," he says before taking the sandwich from me. I open my container of fresh-cut apples and caramel and sit it between us.

"Are there other ways you could track me?"

His sandwich stills halfway to his mouth. "You would let me?" His eyes light up a bit, and he seems excited at the idea.

"I'm not saying no," I tell him, taking a bite of my sandwich. He does the same, and I can see his mind working as if putting something into play already.

I watch him eat, unable to stop looking at the tattoos on his hands. I reach out to touch one before I think better of it. He freezes at my touch on his bare skin and twitches like I've hurt him.

"Does that bother you?" I ask, tracing one of the tattoos on his hand. He looks as if he's searching for an answer, or maybe he doesn't want to give me one. "You flinched," I say, pushing for something.

"I'm used to pain when someone touches me." Once again he says it so easily, like it's no big deal. It's then I know Ivan's life is darker than I ever thought possible, and something about that makes me want to touch him more, slide even closer, show him that isn't true and that there is softness in this world. If you asked my family, they would say I'm the definition of it.

"I'd never hurt you," I tell him.

"I think you could hurt me more than anyone ever has."

My eyes snap to his and we stare at each other. I feel the warm breeze on my cheeks and the sun shining between us. His agonized dark eyes are a stark contrast to what's happening inside me. I feel as if I'm coming alive, bursting into being.

"People are watching. They don't think you belong with me," he whispers.

I look around the school and see he's right. People stare at us, but they have to know he's allowed to be here. No one gets on school grounds without going through the proper protocol.

"It's time to get back to class, *krasota*. I'll be waiting for you after."

Chapter Six

Ivan

It's after three in the morning and I can't sleep. My body is used to it, though. I normally only need a couple of hours and I'm able to function. But I can't pretend the reason I'm awake isn't the green-eyed beauty who sleeps not so far away.

I run my thumb across my phone screen and stare at the messages she sent me.

When I drove her home after school, her sister was there waiting. Pandora and I haven't spoken, but I see the way she looks at me. She's smart, and she knows her twin. I kept my distance and didn't interact with Penelope all evening. I went outside and only watched her from afar until Paige and Ryan came home. Afterwards I went to the guest house and worked out in the gym there.

Around eleven I got the first one.

Penelope: You still awake?

Me: Da.

Penelope: You didn't say goodbye.

Me: I made sure you were safe.

Penelope: That's not the same thing.

Me: I will say goodbye to you from now on.

Penelope: You're very agreeable. ☺

Me: For you, I would agree to many things.

Penelope: Send me a picture.

Me: Almost anything.

I smile at the words, knowing they came from her.

I push out of bed and walk down the hall to the gym again. If I can't settle my mind, I'll hone my body. The room must have been two bedrooms at one point, but a dividing wall was taken down to create a large workout space. Floor-to-ceiling windows span the length of the room, showing a view of the garden separating my house from the main one. Right now, it's bathed in moonlight, and though it should be eerie, it's peaceful.

I don't turn on the overhead light. Instead I let the glow of the moon cast shadows across the floor as I walk barefoot over to the pull-up bars. I'm dressed only in black boxer briefs, but I don't need anything else for what I plan on doing.

I walk over to the long steel beam and jump up, gripping it with both hands. My feet are maybe an inch off the ground and I'm only about a foot from the window. I spread my hands wide, working the muscles in my back and shoulders more. I begin to pull my body up, the burn across my chest and abs tightening. I count out, and after about twenty I feel the sweat start to trickle down my spine. I should stop, but I keep pushing myself, willing the image of those green eyes to stop haunting me. I grit my teeth and grunt, looking beyond the glass and into the trees.

I stall myself halfway into the next rep when I catch a glimpse of something moving. I let go of the bar and drop down to my feet, scanning again to see what it was. It may have been an animal or a trick of the light, but I could have sworn I saw a flash of red.

Stepping up to the glass, my heavy breath fogs up the view. I wait for what seems like a long moment, watching the steam disappear, and as it lifts, I spot her. She's on the edge of the trees that separate the yards, sitting on the edge of the small fountain. Her dark red hair cascades down her back, and her bare shoulder glows in the moonlight. She's wearing a tank top with shorts, and her long, creamy legs are tucked under her. I can see the edge of her delicate toes, and I lick my lips. An ache, deep inside me, longs to kiss her there, to kiss every little curve of her body and caress the hidden secrets beneath her clothes. I've never wanted something so innocent for myself. Before Penelope, I wouldn't have dared ruin something so perfect and pure, but my desire for her is outweighing any honor I held.

I press my hands to the cool glass and whisper the

only name she should ever be called. *Krasota*. As if she hears me, she turns her head, and her eyes search for me. She can't possibly see me in the dark, but in my heart I hope that's what she's doing.

After a moment she turns away, and I ache for her eyes to be on me again. I want to fall to my knees and beg her to look at me for all eternity. I shouldn't want her, I shouldn't feel pain in my chest at the mere thought of her. But I am uncontrolled when it comes to her, and I can't stop myself.

I turn and go to my room, grabbing a T-shirt and a pair of loose shorts on the way. The cotton clings to my body as it soaks up the sweat, but I don't have time to stop and think about it. I hurry, thinking that if she is a dream, any moment she'll disappear into the night and I'll be left with a hole in my chest, a space only she can fill.

By the time I make it outside, my feet are wet from the damp grass. It's then I notice I forgot to put shoes on. I don't bother to go back and get them as I walk around to the fountain, anxious to see if she's still there.

Like a wish from a dream, she's in the same place. The soft light across her body only highlights her beauty.

"It's late," I say, breaking the quiet of the night.

She gasps and turns around, as if shocked to see me standing here. "What are you doing here?"

Her words are not cruel, but they still cut me. Does she not wish for me to be near her? Maybe coming outside to join her was a mistake, even though all of my instincts demanded I go to her.

"Sorry," she says, shaking her head. As if she knows what I'm thinking, she smooths over her words. "I mean, how are you here? You look like you got out of bed. But you're sweaty."

Her eyes roam down my shirt and then to my feet. Her slow perusal of me makes me want to flex my chest to impress her, like some lion in the wild preening for his mate. I want her to feel desire when she sees me.

I can see the barest hint of a blush as her gaze lingers on me, then she lifts her eyes to meet mine.

I take a few steps closer and walk over to the fountain and sit on the edge with her. Not close enough to touch but close enough that my chest isn't hurting.

"Your parents insisted I stay in the guest house. At least until the end of your school year."

"Oh." She turns her head to look in the direction of the house. She stares at the exact spot where I was standing before, and I see her eyes narrow. She looks back to me, but she doesn't say anything further.

"Shouldn't you be sleeping?" I ask, and I see a small smile pull at her lips.

"I couldn't." She shrugs. "I had a lot on my mind." Before I can ask her what, she turns the question to me. "Why are you awake so late? Shouldn't you be sleeping?"

"I don't sleep much." I reach out, running my fingers through the cool water of the fountain. "I was working out and I saw you."

When I look at her again, I see her lick her bottom lip and bite it before nodding. The pain is back, but this time it's lower than my chest. Much lower.

"You didn't send me a picture." Her playful smile makes my blood race, and I want to give her a thousand pictures, anything to keep that look on her face. "Maybe I should take one now."

"It's too dark," I say, looking around, trying to find a way to control my body.

I see her phone beside her and watch as she picks it up and points it at me. I don't look at the camera, though. I only look at her. Her long red hair over one shoulder, the edge of her jaw and high cheekbones. She's more beautiful than any painting I've ever seen, and I could stare at her for eternity.

"There. Now I can add your face on my contacts. I hate not having a picture to go on the little bubble."

"Bubble?" I ask, confused by her statement.

"Yeah, here."

She scoots over right next to me, the side of her body pressed firmly to mine. If I were to wrap my arm around her, she would be enveloped in me, blanketed in my scent. Something primal inside my soul wishes for this, wants to rub my body against hers in a way that marks her as mine. I have to close my eyes tightly to collect myself.

"See, all my contacts have pictures, and before, yours was just a little white bubble. Now there's you. Well, a dark you, but still. It works."

"It's not safe for you out here tonight, *krasota*." The words are out of my mouth before I can stop them. But that doesn't make them any less true.

"Why? Our backyard isn't safe?" She looks around skeptically and then back to me.

I don't know how to tell her that I'm the threat. That everything about her is pulling me in and I don't know how much longer I can control myself. There is a need building, and I can feel the charged air around me grow still. There is only one way to stop this madness, and it's to push her from me. I must put an end to the smiles she gifts me. I don't want to hurt her, but I know my words will.

"You are a young woman, and you have no business being out this late. Your parents would disapprove, and as your security, I demand you leave here and go back to your room." I stand up and take a step away from her.

The pain that flashes across her eyes is almost enough to break me. I open my mouth to take it all back, but she stands up and puts even more distance between us.

"Nobody asked you to come out here and tell me what to do. I was fine until you showed up."

"That makes two of us, *krasota*."

She clenches her jaw, and I long to run my thumb across it, to ease the pain I've caused her and to tell her this is only to protect her, to protect the both of us. But I don't. Instead I remain where I stand, begging her silently to run from me.

"Don't call me that." Her words are sharp as she turns and walks away. But halfway to the house, she looks back over her shoulder. She opens her mouth to speak but changes her mind.

I would give everything in my possession to undo what I just did. I have more money than most people dream of, but it means nothing to me. The only thing that matters is the light in Penelope's eyes, and as she walked away I saw it fade. A piece of me wanted this to happen, knowing it was for the best. But the rest of me is screaming in agony.

As I walk from the fountain and back into the guest house, I think about the look on her face. The light in her eyes that I love had dimmed, but it wasn't gone. It wasn't finished. And as I get into bed and read our earlier text exchange, I know that I'm not, either.

Chapter Seven

Penelope

"What are you doing?" Pandora asks as she walks into her bedroom. She drops her bag on the floor and books spill out.

I'm running on her treadmill. Running always clears my mind, but today that doesn't seem to be working. The hole that I've felt in my stomach won't seem to close. I feel like I'm a ball of anxious nerves, and I don't know what to do with any of it. I'm always the happy one. I never let anything get me down. But today sucked, and I can't keep on the fake smile I've been rocking all day. I've tried to pretend Ivan's words didn't bother me, act like I didn't let a man so easily take my heart and crack it.

"What does it look like I'm doing?" I snap. She raises her eyebrows and holds her hands up in a silent question. I know what she's asking. She likes to run on the treadmill, and I love running outside. But going outside means I need to take my guard with me, and I've been avoiding Ivan all day as best I can.

When he was waiting to take me to school today I didn't slide into the front seat. I went straight for the back, even sitting behind him so I couldn't see him as well. So I couldn't stare at his tattoos and trace them with my eyes. So I wouldn't try to reach out and touch him. I didn't say a word when I stepped past him into the school building. I remained quiet the whole time, which is very unlike me.

Though I did go look to see if he was at the bench today at lunch. He was, so I stayed inside and went to the cafeteria. Why was he at the bench? He'd made it clear last night that he was better off without me in his life and that he was fine before I entered it. I thought he liked me. It doesn't make any sense. The worst part is that for some reason I thought this man would never hurt me. He's a protector, but he let himself cause the harm. The ache still lingers strong with no signs of lessening.

Something about him drew me towards him. I felt like he needed me. I wanted him to need me.

"You ready to talk about it now? I see you've dropped that fake smile," Pandora says, flopping down on the bed, clearly seeing through my act today though she hadn't called me on it until now.

I pull the string on the treadmill and jump off. Pandora moves over on the bed, and I fall back next to her. Her hand slides into mine.

"He doesn't like me," I tell her.

"Bullshit. Everyone likes you. Sometimes it's a little annoying."

Pandora isn't a people person. I walk into a room

and talk to everyone. She avoids everyone like they have the plague.

I roll to my side, looking at her. "How come the first guy I want—"

Pandora cocks an eyebrow at me.

"Okay, okay, I mean *really* want—more than flirting and school or whatever, *really* want—doesn't even want to be around me?"

Maybe it's karma. Pandora always joked that one day someone was going to break my heart.

"I have no idea, to be honest with you. I can't read him. He seems to always have a blank scowl on his face. But I haven't been around him much."

I drop back down on the bed, looking up at the white ceiling.

"It's for the best." She squeezes my hand. "Penelope, that man is dark. He's been through shit. I'm sure that if he told you about it you'd cry and be sad for weeks. You're soft and sweet and all heart. You need someone who can give you those things back."

"I touched him the other day and he flinched. He said he only knows pain from touch," I tell her.

"Fuck," she mumbles.

"Mom and Dad wouldn't bring him around us if they thought he was bad." I don't know why, but I still feel the need to protect him, stand up for him.

"I'm not saying he's bad. I'm saying he's broken." She knocks my shoulder with hers. "I mean, he has to be broken, because no man can ever withstand your charms."

I can't help the small laugh that escapes me.

"Mom and Dad head out for date night?" I ask. They always do date night on Friday. I never cook on those nights, so Pandora and I just snack on stuff instead of making a whole meal.

"Yep," she confirms.

I sit up, letting go of her hand.

"No," she says before I can even get off the bed.

"Come on. I need something to get me out of this funk." Also to keep me distracted so I don't keep checking my phone in hopes he will text me. Tell me he didn't mean what he said. Ask me to come to the backyard.

"No," she says again flatly and doesn't move.

I put my hands on my hips and stare at her. "This is going one of two ways."

"Fucking shit," she mumbles, sitting up. I want to go out and do something, and I clearly don't want Ivan around. She knows that. So that means we're sneaking out. She can come willingly or she'll follow me. But we both know she's not letting me go alone.

"Fine." She rolls off the bed and stands up. "Dancing?" she asks, and I see a small smile pull at her lips. She pretends to hate when we go dancing, but she loves it, and we haven't been in a while.

"God, it's been forever." I smile, feeling a little lighter.

Pandora and I have always loved to dance. I don't think we're any good at it, but we like to jump around and sing as loud as we can to the music, and neither of us care if we make fools of ourselves.

"Okay, I'm getting ready!" I half-scream, running from her room excitedly.

"See you in two hours," Pandora grumbles, making me laugh.

"I'll be fast, I promise. It's already ten," I shout from the other room, flinging open my closet doors.

I grab a gray dress that I know will look great with my hair. I toss it on the bed then run out of my room and towards my mom's. I burst out laughing when I see Pandora already in Mom's closet holding up a pair of black knee-high boots.

"Mine." She holds them to her chest like I might snatch them from her.

"I'm going for these." I grab a pair of black Miu Mius that have diamonds on the heels. They'll not only be easy to dance in but will also go perfectly with my dress.

I turn, dashing back to my room and tossing the shoes next to the dress. Pulling my hair up, I take a quick shower and then get out, rushing to get ready. I towel off and pull my hair down. I don't need to do much with it. I apply some makeup then slip from the bathroom and throw on a matching strapless bra and panties.

Pandora opens my door, leaning against the frame as I pull the dress over my head and straighten it out. It's Grecian-style and ties on one shoulder and bunches at the hip, but it manages to hug my curves perfectly. After I put my shoes on, I turn to look at Pandora. She's dressed like always. Except for when she has to wear a school uniform, she's always in all black. Black boots, tight black pants, and a tight black tee. I know we look the same, but I always feel like black does nothing for me. But with her, I swear it makes her eyes even brighter and her hair a more vivid color.

"You look hot," I tell her. She shrugs like she doesn't care if she does or not.

"That dress is short."

I do the same shrug she just did. It is a little short, but I don't care. I look at myself in the mirror, and Pandora comes to stand next to me.

"No way are they going to ID us," I say, looking over at her for confirmation.

"Let me go first when we get there."

"Got one in mind?" I ask. She always has a club she wants to go to.

"Yep," is all she says, making me smile.

"Let's do this."

I pull out my phone and call for a car. We make our way back towards Pandora's room and go into the bathroom. Pandora slides the little window open and jumps out easily. I take my heels off and toss them out the window then climb up. She helps me jump down, and it's like we've done this a thousand times. Maybe we have.

Pandora's crazy ass somehow figured out how to disable the alarm on her bathroom window a while back, and no one has seemed to notice. We make our way along the house and hurry when we get to the driveway. I pull out my emergency gate key and slide it in, then Pandora and I grab and pull open the heavy gate. We open it just enough to slip out before locking it again. We hurry down the street, where we see our car waiting at the corner.

We jump in, giggling, and I yell at the driver, "Go,

go, go!" I'm acting like someone is actually chasing us. He takes off, and the tires squeal, making us burst out laughing again.

"Take us to Sin." Pandora gives him the address of our favorite dance club, and I sit back, relaxing.

It doesn't take long to get into the city, then we're slipping out of our car. Pandora grabs my hand as she struts to the front of the line. She walks with confidence and purpose. The bouncer at the door lifts the cord and opens the door for us, letting us in, without comment.

"How do you do that?" I whisper over to her.

"You act like you own the place. Besides, twins dressed up for a night out? They're letting us in."

I roll my eyes, but she's probably right. Men have creepy twin fantasies.

As we make our way down a long hallway, the music grows louder and louder. We don't stop for a table or even go to the bar for a drink. We head right for the dance floor. It's the only reason we're here. I let the thrumming bass take me, but my mind still fixes on what Ivan might be doing right now.

Chapter Eight

Ivan

It didn't take me long to follow her. I'd been watching the house ever since Paige texted me that she and Ryan were going on a date. She said Pandora had the alarm off on the window in her bathroom, so if they planned on sneaking out, that's the way they were going.

When I asked her why she didn't put the alarm on, she said it was easier to watch one window than all the other exits in the house.

I got dressed after my workout and put on a pair of dark gray slacks and a button-up shirt. I went and sat outside the gate in my black Porsche 911, waiting to see what would happen. It only took about two hours before I watched the girls sneak out of the gate and make a run for it down to the waiting cab. I caught sight of Penelope laughing and my chest warmed instantly.

As I followed them at a distance, I thought about why I'm so drawn to her. I've been around darkness and dirt most of my life. There were occasions when I met people who were kind, but more often than not, I kept to myself. I knew the shadows and clung to them. But the second I looked at Penelope, I saw light for the first time. She wasn't only innocent and pure. She was untouched in her soul. I knew by looking at her that I would never meet another woman with this kind of love radiating from her.

I'd never seen eyes like hers staring back at me. They were emeralds sparkling with truth, and they saw straight to my core. She never flinched at what she found in there. She touched me, and I felt like she cast a spell. The warmth spread to every inch of my body, coating me in her protection.

Was I really the one trying to keep her from danger? How could she undo me like this and still make me feel like she's holding me together? It's inexplicable, but I want to cling to her light.

I watch as the girls enter the club without being carded. I pull up to the curb, toss my keys to the valet and slip him a bill. "Keep it close," I say in his ear as he glances down at the hundred, and nods.

The bouncer lets me in with the same courtesy he extended the twins. I try not to think about how many other underage people he lets in here.

The music is loud, and almost immediately it's deafening my senses. I ignore it and scan the crowd as I blend into the corners of the room. I don't want her to know I'm here, but I want to make sure she's safe.

It takes only a second to spot the redheads on the dance floor. It's crowded, but they dance together and people leave them alone.

I grit my teeth when the crowd clears enough for me

to see what she's got on. Her dress is so short it nearly exposes the bottom curve of her ass. I walk to the bar, which has a direct view, and order a shot.

She loves to dance.

Her small body moves with the dark beat of the bass as I throw back a shot of vodka. There is no burn as the liquid warmth hits my tongue and melts down my throat. I clench the glass because I can't put my hands where I want them.

The seductive curve of her waist as it cascades to the flare of her hips... I watch transfixed as they move side to side. Side to side. Her body is like the pendulum inside a grandfather clock, and I can't look away.

The music is deafening, but if she were to simply whisper my name, I would be at her feet, begging to touch what I shouldn't, taste what doesn't belong to me, run my hands along the sweet innocence she taunts me with. An innocence I shouldn't want but crave. Something so pure and untouched like nothing I've ever known before.

Slamming the glass down on the bar, I'm both disappointed and relieved when it doesn't break. Maybe the cut of the glass could cool the feelings I have pulsing though me but I doubt it. Not with her. I'm not sure anything ever could. I would welcome a pain that's greater than my ache for her. For there is nothing more powerful than the spell she has me under.

I've been hired to protect her.

But as I push away from the bar and walk towards her, I can't help but think that perhaps someone should have protected her from me.

I watch as Pandora steps away from her and goes to the bar on the other side and grabs a bottle of water. She leans up against the bar, watching her sister as she catches her breath. Penelope still dances, and I can't stand the distance anymore.

The physical distance between us now, and the distance I put between us last night. I hated how she was so cold to me today. It made me miss every part of her, every look in her eyes. I can't have her keeping that from me.

I see Pandora's face when she spots me, and she knows they're busted. But to her credit, she only shrugs and nods towards Penelope. As if it's her fault they're here.

Penelope is facing away from me as I walk onto the dance floor. I don't know the song that plays, but it's slow, and her body knows every beat.

I should grab her and drag her out of here. I should make her go home and explain that this isn't smart or safe. I should do anything but slide my hands to her hips. But that's exactly what I do.

She tenses when I pull her back against my front. I mold her body to mine and press my lips to her ear. "It's me, *krasota*."

She stills again, but I run my hands along her hips and start to move. I don't think she wants to move with me, but she can't stop herself. She loves it too much.

I feel the energy flowing from her, and it passes to me. The music is dark, and the song talks about diamonds. I want to strip Penelope bare and pour them on her. Her skin should only be touched by something worthy of it. Not me. Not my hands. But selfishly I don't take them off her.

Her exposed shoulder and neck are so close that I can see the light sheen of sweat on them. I lean down, and I can smell the scent of lavender mixed with her body. I have to use all of my strength not to lean down and taste it.

Instead I caress her warm curves, giving in to the beast inside me, taking what I want without thought to consequence. I'm an animal when confronted with her delicate tenderness, but she leans back into me. She rubs the swell of her ass across my aching cock, and I moan into her ear. She shivers, and I move my mouth lower, pressing my lips to her neck. I can't stop myself, and I don't know that I care to try anymore.

I kiss across her shoulder and then back up, licking the shell of her ear. I'm out of control, but it feels right. We are lost in this moment, and I don't want it to end.

I look down at her, and she turns in my arms. Her hands press to my chest, and I feel the lower half of her press closer to me, closer to my hardness. She licks her lips and tilts her head up.

"*Potseluy menya.*"

She whispers the words, but they echo in my ears. I should stop and think about what she's asking of me and how she could know Russian. But none of that matters. I simply give her what she asks for.

Leaning down, I place a hand on her neck and feel her pulse against my palm. Her eyes are wide, but not with fear. There is only passion and need, and it matches my own. She closes them as I press my lips to hers, but

I keep mine open. I want to see her when I kiss her for the first time. I want to watch her reaction to me.

I know that I can't let her go and that I won't give her up. I've done bad things in my life, and I don't deserve her. But I can't do the honorable thing when it comes to Penelope. I've never been noble, and I'm not starting now.

When her tongue comes out and touches mine, that's when my eyes close. That's when I'm thrown over the edge and begin the fall.

I can only pray that when I land, I'm still able to catch her.

Chapter Nine

Penelope

I get lost in him, letting the rest of the world melt away. I don't care where I am or what's going on around us. All the anger I had for him moments ago falls from me. I don't know why, but I don't want to hang on to the anger. I can't be mad at him. Deep down I know he's pushing against me because something inside him is making him do it. A slice of guilt runs through me that I didn't push back. I could have fought harder for him, because I know he needs fighting for.

His lips are soft, softer than I would have imagined. His tongue slow and sweet. The kiss is nothing like I thought it would be, but there's more to him than what's on the surface. The only hard thing about him now is the possessive hold he has on me.

All too soon he pulls back and looks down at me. His dark eyes are fiercer than ever. I can't read him. Too much is pushing through. Possession, want, need, hope.

"You're here," I say.

Part of me hoped he would show up. That maybe he

saw us sneak out and followed us. I lick my lips, wanting to see if I can still taste him. I want more. I want the look he's giving me right now to never slip away. He's looking at me like I'm his everything.

"I'm sorry, my *krasota*. I didn't mean the things I said before." He pulls me impossibly closer, like he's afraid I will try to get away from him. I swear I feel a tremble in his hands.

"You didn't mean that you were fine until I showed up in your life?" I try to tease, but the words come out laced with hurt. I hate it because I know he knows hurt, and I don't want it coming from me. I can already tell from the way he's acting now that last night was a lie. I should have seen it and not spent the day ignoring him. I should have only given him sweetness. Being cold isn't like me at all.

"I thought I was." He pauses, running his hand along my exposed neck and shoulder. "But you, Penelope, you make me feel," he whispers into my ear. "Feel something that isn't pain."

He leans down, and I think he's going to kiss me again. Instead he presses his lips against my neck. His warm breath brushes against me, and it's like he's breathing me in. He runs his nose along my collarbone, up to my ear. My eyes fall closed, wanting to only have his touch, to only feel him and nothing else around us. What's he doing to me? I don't understand how someone I only met days ago can be so consuming so quickly.

But here it is, and I don't want to let it go. I want to grab ahold of it.

He needs you, a voice inside me echoes.

Now I'm pulling him closer. I have a feeling Pandora was right. Ivan is dark, but I know I can be his light. I can feel it. I'm his other half.

"You two about done?" I hear Pandora yell next to us, making sure we can hear her over the music. The moment is jerked from us, and I look over at her.

Ivan doesn't release me from his hold. "*Net*. I'll never be done." His Russian accent is thicker now, deeper than before. But he isn't looking at Pandora when he says it. He's looking right at me.

"Well, that's great, Big, Dark and Tattooed, but we're leaving," she tells him. She grabs me by the hand to pull me, but Ivan still doesn't let me go.

"*Krasota* wants to dance. We will leave when she's finished." He finally looks over to Pandora, but then his eyes come back to me. "*Krasota*, would you like to dance more?"

"Fucking shit," I hear Pandora say.

"I want to go," I tell him, hoping if we go that means the two of us get to be alone. I want his mouth back on mine.

"Then we go." His hand slides into mine as he leads me from the club.

The crowd parts to make way for us. For Ivan actually. His big body moves through the swarm with purpose.

"I'll call us a cab," Pandora says.

"I'll take you home."

Pandora tries to fight with him, but Ivan challenges her. "I'm her guard."

"Not for long, you won't be. Wait until our mom finds out you're trying to stick it to my sister. The only thing you'll be guarding is your balls."

Ivan shrugs like he doesn't care for the safety of his balls.

"My sister will keep her mouth shut," I half-growl at Pandora. I know she isn't going to tattle, but she still glares at me. Clearly she's not happy about what's going down.

When we make it outside, he goes over to the valet and is handed his keys. He keeps his hand locked with mine as we walk over to a Porsche. He opens the passenger-side door for me and waits.

I glance over at Pandora, who's standing there with her hands on her hips. "I'll sit on your lap," I tell her. She lets out a deep sigh and gets in the car. I slip in after her, sitting awkwardly on top of her legs. Ivan closes the door then goes around to the other side. I move a little so my back is more towards the door.

When Ivan gets in, he reaches over and pulls the seat belt over both my sister and me, clicking it into place. His hand comes up to brush my cheek for a soft touch before he cranks up the car and pulls away from the curb.

We ride in silence for a moment before Pandora breaks it.

"Fuck it," she finally says, and I roll my eyes. "I'm just going to say it."

Yeah, like she's ever bitten her tongue when there's something she wants to say.

"You're no good for her. I know you see it. Look at her. She's sweet and soft and all that shit. She's like the freaking heart of our family. Hell, I bet you've even killed people before." She snaps the last part, and the air in the car feels like it's alive.

I watch something pass over Ivan's face, and I hate it. I elbow Pandora, hitting her right in the ribs before I place my hand over Ivan's, ignoring Pandora's string of curses. He moves his thumb against mine as he welcomes my touch. His eyes stay on the road, but God I wish I could see them right now. I wonder how many other people have judged him all too quickly. Don't they see the man underneath all the tattoos and scars?

"Do you hear her?" I tell him. Leaning more towards him, I say, "She's trying to tell you all the reasons we can't be together. But I don't care. Do you?" I reach up, rubbing the back of my fingers across the stubble on his face. I know if we really want to be together, my sister will be the least of our battles.

"If you want me, *krasota*, I will forever be yours." He says it so simply, as if I can have ownership over him. He leans into my hand.

"I want you," I tell him. "All of you." I watch tension leave his body. I smile at him, and for the first real time in my life I'm pissed at my sister.

"So, Taco Bell?" Pandora says.

I grit my teeth.

"Are you hungry?" Ivan asks, glancing over at me.

"I'm always hungry," Pandora pipes in like he's talking to her.

"*Krasota*?" he asks, ignoring her.

"I want to go home. With you." I add the last part because I don't want there to be any confusion. I need to be alone with him.

Pandora huffs, and the car grows silent again. I place my hand on top of Ivan's as he drives us home. He pulls up to the gate and keys in the code. He takes us to the front of the house, and I hop out and Pandora follows.

"Ivan, I'm coming with you," I tell him as he gets out of the car. I grab Pandora by the arm and pull her towards the side of the house. "I just need a moment with my sister," I call over my shoulder.

I stop when we make it to her bathroom window.

"I'm sorry," she says before I can even yell at her. "I just worry about you. Don't be mad at me." She reaches up and tucks a strand of hair behind my ear. "We don't fight. I was wrong about him I think," she adds, taking me by surprise. "I watched him when I said those things in the car. He's—"

"Don't." I cut her off. I don't want to hear about how he's broken or whatever it is. That's for me and Ivan to work out. I feel so protective of him. I don't want anyone thinking of him in any way but positive.

"You're already so far gone," she says, studying my face. "I know we always joke about how you take care of us. You're the tender one, but no one gets as angry as you when someone goes after what you love." She leans in, kissing me on the cheek. "I'll sleep in your bed tonight so when Mom and Dad get home they'll think we're both in there," she says before opening the window and slipping in. "Be careful. I don't want to have to kill him," she adds as she climbs in and shuts the window.

I think about her words, about how angry I got when she made a comment that I thought hurt Ivan. It only makes me believe even more that he was meant to be mine.

I don't have to turn around to know he's behind me. I have a feeling that's where he'll always be.

Chapter Ten

Ivan

"I snuck in here when I was younger, but there was only a gym at the time, so it didn't hold much appeal."

Penelope takes my hand and leads me down the hallway to where my bedroom is. I should stop her, take her back to the living room, but where she leads I will follow.

"Then how do you know where I sleep?" I ask as I close the bedroom door behind us.

"Process of elimination." She looks back at me over her shoulder as she slips off her shoes and climbs on the bed. "There are two floors and only one bedroom on this one. You'd be down here to either be close to the kitchen or close to me."

"To you," I admit, not shy about my feelings for her. "I can't think of anything else besides you. I'm loyal to your family, and though this may make me an enemy to your parents, I knew the second I saw you that I'd lay down my life for yours."

"I guess people might call this love at first sight," she says, scooting back to the middle of the bed.

I walk over to the side table and press play on the surround sound. Soft music fills the room from the hidden speakers, and I walk back to the bed.

"I don't care what anyone else calls this." I kick off my shoes and unbutton my shirt, opening the front so that my pale skin and tattoos are exposed. "I know that I've never experienced love before and that the feelings I have now for you are unlike anything I've felt before. My soul was bound to yours the first time we touched. If that is love, then I love you, Penelope. But it feels like more than that. More than one word."

She lies back on the bed as I come over her, her hands pressing to my bare chest. Her fingers burrow under the material of my shirt and smooth down my back then come up again. Her nails score a path as they move.

"Will you make love to me?" Her eyes are pleading as her hands move to my shoulders and neck.

"*Da*. But I will give you pleasure first," I answer, leaning down and kissing her softly.

She reaches up, untying the ribbon on one side of her dress and pulling it down. I help her move it down her body until it's off and she's bared to me in her bra and panties. There are no straps on her bra, so I reach around her to unclasp what's covering her breasts.

When they are exposed, I place a kiss between them. I run my nose along the soft swell of her breasts and then kiss them gently before taking a nipple into my mouth. I suckle her delicately, not wanting to hurt her. My only desire is to give to her the same pleasure she has already given me. The gifts of her love and her body are more than a man like me deserves. I will spend my life trying to correct the balance, for she outweighs all that I am a thousand times over.

She pulls at my shirt, asking for more. I strip off my clothes, leaving only my underwear, unable to deny any demand she makes.

"Sweet flower, have you had a man between your thighs before?" I ask as I kiss her feet and move my hands to her panties.

"No. All I've ever done is kiss."

Her blush shows her true innocence, and my cock grows harder. How can I take such beauty for myself and allow her no other for the rest of her life? I tell myself that no man will love her as I do. No man will make her dreams come true as I can. She will want no one else after she has felt the pleasure I will give her body.

"And if we make love, will you hold my baby inside your womb?" I kiss just below her belly button, where the edge of her panties are. I look into her green eyes as I slide them over her hips, revealing her untouched pussy.

"Oh God," she whimpers as my mouth moves lower, almost to the slit of her sweetness. "Um, I'm not on anything. Can you pull out?"

"*Da*, my sweet *krasota*. And where will you let me spill my seed?" I gently spread her legs apart, opening her lips and seeing her nectar.

"Anywhere," she moans as I kiss her most intimate place.

I make love to her pussy with my mouth, tasting the sweetest fruit I've ever eaten. Her ripe juices drip on my lips, and I drink them down. I press two fingers inside her tight channel and feel the pressure of her innocence squeezing against them. My other hand goes inside my underwear to my cock, rubbing it with promises of what's to come. It's the only way I can find relief for the pain that grows unbearable.

When her body tightens and her legs become restless, I know she's approaching her peak. "Stop resisting, my beauty. Do not fight what I give your body."

I press my fingers against the tender place inside her, the spot of pleasure that will be the greatest for her. Then I suck her clit and wait for her to give in. I only have to wait a moment before she can no longer challenge what is happening to her. But because of the struggle, the climax is all the sweeter.

Her honey drips onto my tongue, and I moan as she does. Her cries are loud and her grip on me is tight. My name on her lips is enough for me. I could stop now and hold her all night with that as my only pleasure. My *krasota* saying my name as her orgasm wraps around her body is my vision of heaven. She has given it to me without inhibition, and I will forever be changed because of it.

I rest the side of my cheek on her thigh and close my eyes. I want the memory of this branded into my mind so that when I am one hundred years old, this is still just as perfect.

"Holy shit," Penelope exclaims, and I open my eyes to see her smiling.

"Did you enjoy it?" I ask as I lick my fingers and move up her body.

"Wow." She closes her eyes and lets out a small laugh. "Can you do that again?"

"As many times as you wish, my *krasota*." I wrap my arms around her and kiss her softly.

But she deepens it. Her tongue meets mine, and the flavor of her pussy is warm and sweet between us. There is urgency from her, but I don't want to rush this moment.

"We have forever," I whisper against her lips and rub my nose against hers. "Do not rush me."

Reaching down I slip off my boxer briefs and then run the length of my cock against her slickness. I don't push inside, just lazily coat myself in her honey.

"You feel big," she says, her eyes wide with uncertainty and excitement.

"We will fit, my love. Your body is small, but I will be gentle."

"I love you, Ivan." She touches my cheek and smiles so sweetly at me.

"My heart is in your hands, *krasota*."

I press the head of my cock to her opening and push in slowly. Her warmth hugs me, enveloping the large tip. When I feel her tense, I run my hand across her chest and hard nipples. I kiss her deeply again, letting her relax as I sink even deeper.

She doesn't tense again, but having my cock inside her is new and foreign for her. Her pussy is adjusting, and I try to make it pleasurable as she learns what I feel like when we make love.

I let her soft cunt memorize every ridge of me so that

the next time she will welcome me home. Like the beloved loyal man at her feet, I will await her beckoning.

When the kiss is so great that she needs to catch her breath, I move my lips to her neck and begin to move. I bury my face there as I give her long, slow thrusts of my cock.

"Ivan," she whispers, and it's almost my undoing.

I thrust harder, letting her feel my strength. In this moment, I am possessing not only her body but her spirit. There is a power that moves between us, and her soul now belongs to me.

"Sweet *krasota*, you are my love." I kiss her fiercely, setting this moment in stone. My ownership of her isn't to be taken lightly. It is my solemn vow to be her soldier. The knight in shining armor her little heart dreamed of.

I move a hand to her pussy to tease her tiny bud. I bring my thumb back to my mouth and lick it, then replace it where she needs it most. I want the taste of her innocence on my mouth as she climaxes for me.

I watch a blush blossom on her chest and move up her neck. Her eyes close tight and her head tilts back as once again she stops the fight. She gives in to my gift and falls over the edge of paradise. A sheen of sweat dampens her skin, and we are slick together. Her orgasm is the most beautiful thing I have ever seen, so unrestrained and pure. There is nothing held back when she allows herself this moment.

It takes all the strength I have not to spill my seed within her warmth. It would have been so easy, but I will always do what my *krasota* asks.

Pulling out my cream-covered cock, I sit up and

stroke it while looking down at her nakedness. Her perfect skin, rosy with pleasure, her round breasts with hard nipples begging for more attention.

Her eyes widen as she watches me, and then she brings her own hand to mine. Her soft fingers interlace with mine, and together we stroke my cock. She licks her lips, and I want to come on them, covering the swollen petals with my seed.

But the look of her on her back, legs spread and open for me is too much. Instead, I choose to mark her body, letting her watch me climax onto her.

She pumps me to release, and thick spurts of my love for her land on her pale skin. I watch as each throb brings more, and I reach down, rubbing it in. The yards of unmarked perfection now proudly display my ownership. There has never been a moment where I have felt such complete devotion.

I nearly collapse on top of her and feel the warmth spread between us. I feel as if my entire world is in my arms.

"I don't think I can breathe," she says, and holds me tighter.

"The love is heavy between us. But do not worry, my sweet beauty. I will carry it for the both of us."

Chapter Eleven

Penelope

I lie on my back in the center of Ivan's bed, still naked after our lovemaking. My whole body feels like it's still tingling. His face rests on my belly as his arms wrap around me so tightly I'm a little surprised I can breathe. His hold on me is tight, but I love it.

I run my fingers through his short hair, looking over his back and the tattoos there. I wonder what some of them mean. I only know a few Russian words based on the small amount of reading I've done.

"Ivan, do you have a family back home?"

"There is only you, *krasota*," he says before his lips brush my stomach. The short stubble on his face rubs against my skin. "You are so soft," he says before kissing me again. He can't stop touching me. Every caress lingers like he doesn't want to let me go, as if I'm the most precious thing he has ever held.

I've always felt loved by my family. Their love for me has never been in doubt. But I have always been the one to take care of everyone. Even if it was never asked of me, it's just how I am. I can't help it, and I know they appreciate it. With Ivan, I feel like taking care of him would be so different.

His words are sweet and they make me want to smile and cry for him. He doesn't have anyone. It makes me cherish my family even more. I couldn't imagine my life without them. To try and picture growing up all alone just isn't possible. Maybe that's why he pushed me away yesterday. He's not used to having someone. He doesn't know how to deal with it. But I think that has passed for him, if the hold he has on me now says anything at all.

"Ivan." I move a little under him. His dark eyes come up to meet mine. He raises his head from my stomach when he sees the tears in my eyes.

"Why do you cry?" Concern coats his expression as he leans up over me. His eyes search my face, and tension fills his muscles at my distress. "Did I hurt you?"

"I cry for you," I tell him, reaching up to touch his face as I think about this man being all alone and how he'll never be alone again.

"Don't be sad for me." A smile lights up his face. "Today is the happiest day of my life." He leans down, taking my mouth in a slow, deep, hungry kiss. I try to wrap my legs around him, but the man is too big. I shift under him, still feeling our passion from before. His hardness rubs against me, making me moan into his mouth. I didn't know something like this could be real. The feelings I'm having are so overwhelming. I think I'm going to love being in love.

He pulls back. "You should rest," he tells me. I don't

want to rest. All too soon the sun will rise and I'll have to go back to my own room. "Are you sore?"

"I'm okay," I admit. There's only a twinge of pain left, but I would push through it to make love to him again. "I don't want this night to end. I don't want to go back to my room."

"You don't have to do anything you don't want to." His words are so easy, like we won't have to deal with my parents. He brushes a few of my curls out of my face.

"My parents, they're—"

"You're an adult. You want to stay at my side, I will make it so." He leans down, burying his face in my hair and neck, rolling a little to the side and wrapping around me tightly as our arms and legs tangle together. He's proving his point that I'm not going anywhere. "You want to stay with me, *da*?" I feel him tense at his own question.

"Forever," I tell him.

He mutters something in Russian, but I don't understand it. "I will be good to you always. I promise this. You give me your heart and I swear it will be my life's goal to make you happy."

"What about you? Shouldn't it be my life goal to make you happy as well?"

"*Krasota*." He brings his lips to my neck and kisses me. "If I have you, I will always be happy. But I think you also fail to see all you ever try to do is make everyone happy. You are Mother Angel."

"You're so sweet." I turn on my side, wanting to look at him. I bring my hand up to his face. Maybe I'm just as needy with touches as he is. "Ivan, will you tell me about you? We don't really know a lot about each other," I admit.

"I know all about you."

"I'm sure." I don't even ask. My parents probably told him about me when he was assigned to guard me. He slides one of his hands to my hip and lazily strokes me back and forth.

"Tell me," I push.

"I will tell you anything you ask, my *krasota*, but my life isn't pretty and nice. It's dirty, and I do not wish to soil your mind with such things."

"Is this why you pushed me away yesterday? That—" My words trail off. God, that hurt so much. I didn't know something could hurt like that.

"You are too good for me. I worry that…" He breaks eye contact for a second, as if trying to get his words right. "I will tell you if you wish to stay with me. I will make it happen. I feared letting you close would drag me into you more and that maybe if you ever didn't want to be by my side, I wouldn't allow you to go."

"Maybe I don't want you to ever let me go," I confess. Something about his dark words warm me. I like it. I know I shouldn't. They should scare me, but that's the last thing I'm feeling. His eyes seem to darken at my words.

"Don't move," he tells me, sliding from the bed. I sit up and watch him go over to a dresser. He opens the top drawer and pulls something out then comes back to the bed. I sit up, not caring about my nakedness with him. If anything, he's made me feel even more beautiful with the way he worships my body.

He slides a necklace over my head and drops it down around my neck. The chain is simple, like one they use in the military for dog tags, but on the chain is a thick black ring.

"You said I could track you, *da*?" he says.

I pick up the ring and look at it. The band is a black metal, but smooth and thick. I shrug. "I don't care," I say.

I watch relief wash over his face.

"If it makes you feel—" He cuts me off as his mouth takes mine in a kiss. I'm flat on my back with him over me once again.

He pulls back. "I made it myself, but I will make you a better one as soon as I have the time."

"This one is perfect," I tell him. This is the one he put on me. It's the one I want to wear.

"*Net, krasota*, you are perfect."

Chapter Twelve

Ivan

"I want to talk to you," I say, lightly knocking on the office door.

Paige looks up from her computer and nods. "I've wondered when we would have this conversation."

Her knowing eyes scan the area behind me, but I shake my head and close the door. "I wanted to speak to you alone."

"I'm guessing Penny doesn't know you're talking to me."

"A mother misses nothing, does she?" I say, sitting down across from her.

"Not me. And not when it comes to my babies."

"I love Penelope and I want to marry her. You and I have a long history, and I don't want to see that broken. So I'm coming to you now."

She narrows her eyes at me and crosses her arms. "You come to me after the fact, Ivan. We all knew when you saw her what was happening."

Paige stands up and walks over to the window. It looks out at the garden that separates the guest house from this one. She's quiet for so long I don't know if she's going to speak again. But I wait, and eventually she sighs.

"You're just like him." She turns to look at me over her shoulder and then returns her attention to the window. "Captain always had a pretty face he could hide behind. His true darkness was hidden. But you, Ivan, yours is on display for the world to see."

She walks over to a picture of the family on the wall and looks at it, smiling. "He was born in Russia. Did you know that? I think if he hadn't been adopted he could have easily gone down the same path as you."

I remain silent, wanting to let Paige speak, needing to hear her words before I try to convince her that I'm good enough for her daughter. When her eyes turn to me again, I see fierce protection there, a mother guarding her young.

"If I didn't trust you, you would have never been her guard to begin with. It's because I know deep down you're just as good as she is. But she is the light of our lives. Penelope is different than the rest of us. Pandora is like Captain and me. She's strong, and I never worry about her. Penelope has always had a soft heart."

"*Da*. She is too good for me," I agree.

"Penelope is the kind of woman that will need someone with shoulders big enough to carry her. A man with strength enough to hold her and his family together."

I nod, comfortable in the knowledge that I am that man. I was placed on this earth to do exactly what Paige is asking me—to keep her safe and protect her purity of heart.

"Will you ever let her go?"

"Never," I answer sharply.

"I wanted better for my daughters. I made sure they had a better childhood, a better life, everything better than what I had. But I never envisioned a love better than the one I have with Captain. Because there's nothing more than what I have with him. What we share, what we've made is the only thing I've ever wanted for my girls."

"You're right," I say, sitting up. "I see the two of you, and there is no doubt that what you have with your husband is rare. It's soul mates living side by side. And it's what I have with Penelope."

Paige looks at me and nods.

"I love her, and I will love her until the end of this life and the thousands that follow." I stand up and walk over to Paige. "I would like your blessing and Ryan's to marry Penelope. It would honor us and our love."

"Let me talk to him. He's not going to take it well." She laughs and closes her eyes, shaking her head. "But you have my blessing, Ivan. I knew she was a goner for you from the beginning. And I can't say she didn't get that from me."

Paige shrugs and looks back at the family photo. "Just do me a favor, okay?"

"Anything," I say, standing at attention.

"Promise me you won't take her away from us."

There is a pain in my heart at her words. "The reason I love Penelope is because she's afternoon sunshine and the first blossom of spring. She smells like warm cookies and laughs like an angel. I would never do anything to stop that. I don't want to put her in a box and seal her away. Her family is important to her, and so it's important to me."

Paige nods, and I can see a little relief in her eyes.

"I will never take her from any of you. I wish only to become a part of what you have built."

Paige reaches out and squeezes my shoulder, and if I'm not mistaken there are small tears in her eyes.

"I know that feeling all too well."

A few hours later, when I get back to the guest house and slip back into bed, my *krasota* is still sleeping. I lie there watching the sunlight spread across her shoulder. The sheets are tucked around her waist, and her pale skin glows. Hours pass, and I never take my eyes off her. I could spend the rest of eternity just like this and die a happy man.

When she opens her eyes and smiles at me, the light catches the diamond on her finger, sending prisms of rainbows dancing across the room.

I bought it after I talked with Paige. The five-carat princess-cut pink diamond is surrounded by small white ones on a platinum band. My *krasota* deserves a ring as beautiful as she is, and she will forever be my darling love.

"Ivan," she says, looking at it in shock.

"Will you marry me?"

"Yes!" she screams, throwing herself at me. She giggles with excitement and climbs up my body, wrapping her legs and arms around me as tightly as possible.

I laugh with her and rub my hands down her back. We stay like that for a long time, but we can't remain in our bubble forever.

"Pandora," she says, looking into my eyes.

I nod in understanding. She needs to talk to her twin.

Chapter Thirteen

Penelope

I slip into my room to see Pandora still asleep in my bed. On the weekends she could sleep forever if we let her. Normally her growling stomach is the only thing that motivates her to get up. Crawling onto the bed, I lie next to her and run my finger down her nose. Her face scrunches and she slaps at my hand, making me giggle.

I knew Pandora was the first person I wanted to tell. I know I'll have to face my mom and dad soon enough. Pandora and I share everything, and I hope that she'll be happy for me. I want her to be excited with me. I run my finger down her nose again.

"You better have food," she grumbles, smacking at my hand again. Her eyes fly open when her hand makes contact with my ring. She grabs my hand, looking at the gigantic rock Ivan put on me.

"Never one to waste time are you, Penny?" I hear the laughter in her voice. The little bit of tension I wasn't even aware I was carrying melts away. "It's beautiful."

"Thank you," I tell her, feeling a little choked up now. "I know some might say it's fast."

"Fast is putting it lightly," she laughs. "Seems to be the way this family works, though."

We both smile at that. Dad always talks about how he fell in love with Mom after just one look. Knew from the moment he saw her she would be his life. Then he did anything and everything to make her his.

"I knew the day would come when we'd have to detach ourselves from each other. But I thought we still had more time."

I stare at her, thinking about not having her crawl into my bed every night. I don't know why I didn't think about it before. Things will change between us.

"Ahh, Penny, don't cry. All I'm saying is I'm going to miss you. But it's time for a new Chapter in our lives. I'm just glad you have someone with you in your new chapter."

"What about you? Do you want someone?" I ask.

Something flashes across her face before it's gone. "Just because you're lovestruck doesn't mean you need to push it on me. I think I'll go along with Henry and do the no-dating thing."

I roll my eyes at the mention of our cousin. Henry refuses to date. He said he didn't want to end up all crazy in love like his own parents. Both of our dads seem to have stalker tendencies when it comes to their wives. Henry is terrified he's going to catch it.

"Will you tell Mom and Dad with me?"

The ball of tension in my stomach has suddenly returned. She runs her hands over her face and now I can see she's worried, too. I always get sick when I think about my parents being mad at me. Pandora had always been quick to take the brunt of whatever we got ourselves into as kids. But this time, it's on me. And I need her support.

"How about I tell them I'm knocked up. When they start to freak, we'll just say that we're kidding and Penny's marrying the guy who looks like he murders people for breakfast." I smack her arm, and then she sobers. "Wait, you're not pregnant, are you?"

I roll my eyes at her because she's being crazy—how could I possibly be pregnant already?—but then hers narrow on me.

"All right. Let's go pull this Band-Aid off before you make yourself sick worrying about it. Then you can make me breakfast." She adds the last part as we get out of bed.

Pandora grabs my hand. "If that man is broken, no one will be able to heal him like you."

Her words take me by surprise, and I squeeze her hand. "Thank you."

When we enter the kitchen, Pandora and I both freeze. My dad is staring at Ivan, and my mom is standing in between them. Ivan doesn't move. The look on his face is unreadable, but I know without a doubt my parents are now aware of our relationship. I can feel the tension in the room.

Eventually, Ivan's eyes come to mine, and I watch his whole face soften.

Mom looks over to Pandora and me, and Dad follows her line of sight. His attention goes straight to my finger. I make no move to cover the ring.

"Penelope," my dad says, and I stand at attention.

"Watch your tone," Ivan says.

"Oh shit," Pandora mumbles next to me. No one corrects Dad. Well, no one except Mom.

Dad's attention snaps back to Ivan, who's still staring at me like he didn't just poke a giant bear. It's then I notice that both of them are about the same height. It would be an almost even match, size wise.

"Are you hungry, *krasota*?" Ivan asks me, as if the room isn't about to explode with tension.

"You've got food?" Pandora asks, and I smack her arm. Then I hear my mom snort.

"You don't tell me how to talk to my daughter," my dad says, ignoring everyone but Ivan.

"*Krasota* is precious. No one will talk to her in a way that is not polite."

"All right, I see why you fell for him so fast. He gets food and says shit like that."

I have to bite my lip to keep from smiling at Pandora's words.

My dad takes a deep breath as if to get himself under control. "I know she's precious." My dad looks at me as my mom moves next to him. I'm a little shocked at how calm and okay she seems with all of this. But she might have already known. She knows everything.

My dad instinctively wraps an arm around her. "Is this what you want?" he asks me.

"I love him," I admit.

"Of course you do." He lets out a deep breath. "Okay."

"Okay?" Pandora and I say in unison.

"Penny." Dad says my name a lot softer this time. "It's just hard to take all this in. You're my little girl. You love with your whole heart, and I don't want to see you hurt."

"I would never hurt Penelope." Ivan walks over to me, wrapping an arm around my shoulder, and Dad's eyes narrow for a moment.

"That might be so, Ivan, but we're still going to have a talk about this."

I smile up at Ivan. Dad just gave his approval in a roundabout way. I feel like a weight has been lifted from my chest. I don't even know why I was so worried. I know at the end of the day my family would never stand in the way of my happiness. Maybe it's more that I want them to like him. I want Ivan to be a part of this family. I want him to get a taste of how wonderful having a family really is.

"*Da*, after *krasota* eats."

"I'll make breakfast," I announce.

"Thank God," Pandora says, walking over to the breakfast bar and sitting down.

Ivan leans down and kisses me on the top of my head before letting me go. I walk over to my mom and dad. "You want something, too?"

My dad ignores my question, pulling me into them as they both wrap their arms around me in a tight hug.

"I love you," my dad says.

"Let me see the ring," Mom demands. "Looks like someone wants to make sure everyone within a mile knows you're taken."

I feel myself blush a little as she smiles at me.

"I'm going to starve to death," Pandora whines, and I roll my eyes.

Ivan takes a seat at the breakfast bar as I start to cook. He watches me the whole time.

I take a coffee over to him and set it down in front of him. He holds my hand and runs his thumb across my knuckle. "I love you, *krasota*," he says, bringing my hand to his mouth and kissing it.

"I love you, too," I reply, watching a smile pull at his lips. His whole face changes so much when he smiles.

"Let's talk about this wedding," I hear my mom say. I look over at her and she's smiling. My dad is glaring at Ivan's hand holding mine.

Pandora lets out a sound like she's dying, and her head drops to the countertop. "Oh my God, she's going to make me wear a dress!"

"Oh my God, I get to plan a wedding!" I squeal with excitement.

"This is going to be hell," Pandora grumbles, but when she lifts her head to look at me she's smiling.

Then I look around the room and I notice everyone is smiling.

I feel myself start to tear up from the amount of happiness flowing through me. It's overwhelming to have this much love in one room, but I wouldn't want it any other way. I know that from this day forward, my family is growing. Not only by adding Ivan, but in our hearts.

And now the next Chapter begins.

Epilogue

Penelope

A few months later...

"*Krasota*," Ivan moans into my neck as we both come. His warm release fills me, and I hold on to him tighter, wanting to stay lost in the moment. Lost in him.

"I'm sorry, *krasota*. My control is not strong after last night."

My eyes open lazily at his words. His dark ones meet mine. He leans in, taking my mouth in a soft kiss. When he pulls back I smile because I got lipstick on him. I should probably tell him, but I like the idea that I left a mark on him.

"I missed you, too, and never be sorry," I tell him.

Pandora and Mom made me have a sleepover last night, saying the bride isn't supposed to be with the groom the night before the wedding. Ivan and I reluctantly agreed, but I was glad I did. Spending my last unmarried night with my sister and mom was a memory I will always cherish.

I don't think Ivan did, though, and I have a feeling he'd been waiting for a moment to pounce on me. This has been the only moment I've been alone in the last twenty-four hours. He popped out of nowhere to push up my dress and pin me to the nearest wall. I knew he'd been watching and waiting. It made me smile even more.

"What the hell?" I hear Pandora yelp as she tries to open my bedroom door. "Ivan better not be in there!" she yells. I have to fight a giggle, and even Ivan smiles.

He's grown closer and closer to my family each day. He's been giving me more of himself and telling me pieces about his life in Russia. I love that he's just as much a part of this family as the rest of us, and I know he likes it, too. Pandora is always poking at him and making jokes. At first I used to get all pissy about it, thinking she was being a little mean to him. But then I realized she does the same thing with Henry, and I know that's her way of accepting him as one of us. I even caught Ivan laughing with her when she does it. He can give pretty good, too.

"My *krasota* is here, so of course I am here," he yells through the door. He's poking at her, and I roll my eyes.

"Put me down," I whisper to him. He lets out a deep sigh, clearly not liking the idea. "The sooner I'm ready, the sooner I belong to you forever," I remind him.

"You already belong to me. And me to you," he adds, making me smile at him.

"And the sooner we can be off on our honeymoon, where it's just you and me for three whole weeks."

"Open this door," Pandora growls, jerking the handle.

Ivan pulls back, his cock slipping free and making me moan. His eyes darken, and I know he wants to take me again. I feel his release start to run down my thighs as he places me on my feet. The sight catches his eye, and he reaches for me. I have to jump away from him before I'm pinned to the wall again. My dress falls down and covers me up again.

Ivan rights his clothes as I unlock the door. Pandora comes barreling in, her red hair a wild mess. She glares at Ivan for a moment before she looks at me. "You messed up your makeup."

"She looks perfect," Ivan tries to correct her.

"Since when do you care about makeup?" I ask. It's funny how much Pandora has been into this wedding. She's been running around barking orders at people, making sure everything is getting done. In her defense, I'm not as good at snapping at people as she is.

I already got upset about the invitations being printed wrong. I tried to say something to the company that made them, but they blew me off. I told Pandora about it because I knew if I told Ivan he'd probably burn their building down. She seemed the safer bet, but after that she kind of took over. She clearly did not like the idea of someone trying to push me around.

"Since you had to have three dresses for your wedding day?" she throws back at me, not really even answering my question.

"I needed them!" I snap back. My wedding dress, my after-party dress, then the dress I'll leave in. This seems completely reasonable to me. "You have an outfit change, too," I say accusingly.

"Because I'm not wearing a dress all day." She glances over at Ivan. She's probably wondering what he's still doing here. "Don't you need to be getting ready?"

He merely shrugs. He won't leave until I say something.

"Okay, okay. We'll get ready," I tell her, going back over to Ivan. He leans down, giving me a kiss. "I'll see you soon, my *muzh*," I tell him, calling him "husband" in Russian. Over the last few months I've picked up a lot of it.

He cups my face, kissing the tip of my nose before turning to leave.

Afterwards I look at Pandora, who has a wistful look on her face. The look catches me off guard, and I wonder if all her talk about not wanting a man is bullshit.

We both start college soon. It will be the first time we are really apart. She's moving into the city to go to school, and I'm staying out here and taking some classes online. My aunt Mallory has been pushing me towards accounting, and I'm starting to think that's what I want to do.

I think Ivan is making a business out of his tracking devices. He's always coming up with cool ideas of what to put them into. Maybe I could help on the business side of that. Mom and Dad already have him making stuff for them for work.

"That man loves you. I feel like an ass that I ever tried to stand in the way of that," Pandora finally says.

I walk up to her and grab her hand. "Then promise me something."

"Anything," she responds instantly.

"That when the day comes and you fall in love, *you* don't stand in *your* own way."

She stares at me for a moment like she's thinking it over.

"Okay, I promise," she says after a beat. "Not that I think that day will ever come," she adds, and I shake my head.

"Okay, enough about me. We need to get the show on the road so Dad can walk you down the aisle. Mom and I have bets on how long it will take him to let you go when you get to the end." She leans in close. "I bet ten seconds, so do your sister a solid."

I laugh.

"For real, though, let's do this thing. I don't know how much longer Dad can hold Ivan back. The man already gave him the slip once."

That makes me smile even more because I love the idea of Dad and Ivan hanging out. They have become close, my dad treating him at times like his own son. God, my family couldn't be more perfect. They always say I'm the heart of this family, but in truth, it takes us all to make it beat.

Epilogue

Ivan

Ten years later...

Penelope comes running into the room and jumps into my arms. I laugh as I kiss her lips and carry her to our bedroom.

"Are you happy, *krasota*?"

"Happier than I ever dreamed possible."

"Are you happy because our children are next door spending the night?" I smile at her and rub the stubble on my chin against her neck.

She giggles and then snorts as I drop her on the bed.

I hover above her, looking down at my beauty. The years have been a gift to her, because she is more beautiful with each passing day. The way she's grown soft in her belly and the way her hips have widened... There is nothing more stunning than seeing my wife round with our little babies. We've had two, and she says no more. She says that we are blessed with one boy and one girl and that we are lucky.

I am the lucky one. To have Penelope choose me as her mate, as her lover, for all of our days is the dream come true.

We have made a family together, a life more precious than I could have imagined. After we were married she asked to live near her family, so naturally I built her a home next door to them. I will always give my *krasota* what she wishes.

Now Pandora and her family live on the other side of us. We are one big compound of babies and babysitters. Penelope loves nothing more than mothering us all and was quick to become a stay-at-home mom. People joke and say we have a village, but I don't see this as a bad thing. We are a family, and that's something I never dared to hope for. But as years have passed, Penelope has made me understand that it is good to hope.

"I'm happy to have you alone for the night. Even if it's only for a few hours before the kids try to sneak back over here."

I pull off her sundress and sandals, kissing her feet. My mouth moves higher as her legs fall open for me.

"Do you wish for my kisses?" I ask, looking into the green eyes that hold my heart.

"You know I do." She winks at me, raising her hips in invitation.

"Then you shall have all of them."

I move my mouth between her legs and kiss her sweet nectar until she climaxes. We've been together ten years, and as I sink into her I think about how it's always special. Every time we connect there is love—love of our bodies, love of our spirits, love of our souls.

She wraps her arms around my neck, and I pull her body flush with mine.

"Stay close," she whispers, and I obey.

I hold her tight as I thrust in and out, leaving no space between us.

It's hours later when she's sated, and I wrap my body around hers. There are no more words, only kisses and light touches as she drifts off to sleep. I hum softly to her, the same tune I sang to our babies. She closes her eyes, and her dark half-moon lashes make her look like a doll, so perfect and sweet as she sleeps on my chest.

Although my life began dark and lonely, I am thankful for it. I would charge down any path that led to the love next to me, that brought me home to the happily ever after we have built. My beauty has taught me many things, but believing in fairy tales was the most important one. She shows me every day that dreams do come true.

* * * * *

HOLD TIGHT

To sisters... By blood or by choice,
we couldn't do life without you by our sides.

Prologue

Royce

My friends call me Rolly. Granted, I used to be chubby when I was a kid, but I grew out of that around ten. The reason it started is because I come from a long line of rich assholes. The Davenport name is known all over New York, and my father is no exception. I went to one of the most expensive private schools in the state, and when I showed up with the name Royce, it wasn't hard to connect the dots to Rolls Royce. Rolls turned into Rolly, and that was that. It stuck from day one, and though most of the kids I grew up with ended up being douchebags, a couple of them were ride or die.

My two buddies and I got out of college and started up a consultancy firm. We used the money we made from hustling. The only things we wouldn't do to make it was sell drugs or ask our parents for it. My buddies, Ezra and Donovan, came from the same background as me, and the three of us agreed we wanted to be our own men. It sucked living in a four hundred square foot studio with two mattresses pushed together and a bathroom with no door. But we made it big in less than five years.

I wanted to make my own contacts, and when I met Henry Osbourne at a charity function last year, I knew that working with him would benefit the both of us. What I didn't know was that the day he asked me to come take a look at his departments was the day she would walk into my life.

Pandora was unlike any woman I'd ever seen. Her red hair was pulled back from her face, and her dark blue eyes were rimmed with black eyeliner. It made her look intimidating. And sexy as fuck. She was petite, but I got the impression from her stance—and from her handshake—that she could take me down in the blink of an eye. God, she had no idea how much I wanted her to try.

They say that like recognizes like, and the day I looked into her deep blues, I met my other half. She was my equal in every way—possibly even better than I'm willing to admit. I had to have her. Plain and simple. Too bad it wasn't that easy.

Chapter One

Pandora

"I swear on every bagel in Manhattan that if you come over here and ask me what time you can go to lunch, I'll burn this building to the ground."

The new guy, Josh, looks at me with a blank expression on his face and takes a step back. "So, um, now?"

"Go to lunch. Before she kills us all," Sophia says, patting him on the shoulder.

He walks away, and I drop my head on the desk. I want to beat it against it, but I don't want the mark on my forehead for the rest of the day. It would be too much of a reminder of my frustration.

"Sorry. I meant to intercept before he got to you. How's it going, boss?"

I lean up from my desk and sit back in my chair. "I'm still not used to you calling me *boss*." I smile at Sophia, and she shrugs.

"Hey, you earned it. Might as well wear the title with honor." She lays a file down on my desk. "That's the

Miller report you asked for. Are you taking a lunch-break today?"

I'm already opening the file and shaking my head as she tells me she'll bring me back something from the cafeteria. I scan the documents and start clicking on my computer to see if I can code some of it now.

An email pops up from my twin sister, Penelope, and I smile. Of course there are pink hearts in the subject line.

I skim it and see she's excited to find out the sex of her baby, and Ivan is being extra protective, but she's so happy she can't seem to care.

Shaking my head, I send an email back, telling her I still think it's a boy and I'll finally be able to have something in common with one of her kids.

Penelope and Ivan got married when she was eighteen. They started having babies right away, and now she's on number three. Ten years later and she's got two beautiful girls, who are full-blown princesses, and one on the way. Fingers crossed this one likes to get dirty.

At twenty-eight, I've got a very different life than my sister. She lives next door to our parents, and they have this big family compound. I've got a place there, too, but I stay in the city most of the time. After college I went in for an internship in the security department at Osbourne Corp. It didn't hurt that my cousin Henry was running the place now, but I'm damn good at my job. I worked my way up, and when the time came for my dad to retire, I was chosen as his replacement. I thought that there may have been some animosity in the department, but I found out afterward that my dad put it to a secret vote so that everyone had a chance to be honest and have the leader they wanted. He said every vote was for me but one. And that one was his. I know I'll always be his little girl, so I couldn't even be mad about it.

I work eighty-hour weeks and give everything I have to this job. I want the department to be the best it can be, but I'm only one person.

Human resources restructured security a few months ago, and we're having some growing pains. Mostly in my ass. Some of the new hires they sent are completely incompetent, and most days I'm spending even more of my time cleaning up their messes.

Henry keeps promising me that he's going to sort it out, but he's running out of time. I'm at my wits' end with trying to manage a department and trying to hold the hands of dumbasses. Good thing personnel can't hear my inner thoughts.

I'm so caught up in my work that at one point I look down and see a bag of food on my desk. I glance up at Sophia, and she shakes her head, laughing. "Thank you," I mouth from across the room.

I inhale the sandwich and the Diet Coke, and it's hours later when I realize that everyone is gone for the day. I heard people telling me goodbye as they were leaving, but it didn't register. Glancing down at the clock on my computer I'm shocked to see it's after ten.

I pull out my phone and see I've got a missed text from my friend Delilah.

Del: I'm at Lincoln's until midnight.

I grab my bag and make my way out of the building, waving to the late-shift staff at the front desk in the lobby. They all know me by first name and watch out for me when I let the time slip by.

As I walk, I respond to the other texts I missed during the day. I send one to thank my mom for sending me the name of the new restaurant that popped up near my apartment, and then I reply to my dad to say that yes, I promise to come home this weekend and see everyone. They like to nag, but I love it. We are all really close, but they know I'm addicted to my job.

I check the rest of my texts on the four-block walk to the bar off the alley. Lincoln's is tucked away and quiet, but they've got a good liquor list and food until three in the morning. What more could a working woman need?

I've got on a black jacket and black slacks with black heels. This is the extent of my entire wardrobe, and it makes me blend into a place like this. When I walk in, I spot Delilah by the pool table and make my way over. We met during the intern program at Osbourne, but she ended up taking an offer at another firm after our year was up. I couldn't blame her. They were willing to make her lead of her own team right away, and that's what we were both after. It was an unspoken competition, and one I'm glad didn't end our friendship.

Her straight dark hair is to her shoulders, and she's got on the same kind of dark suit I have. She's taken off her jacket, and I do the same, revealing my black tank top under it. I see two beers sitting on a table next to her, and I raise an eyebrow.

"Yours should still be cold. I asked the waitress to

bring it about ten minutes ago," she says, racking the balls again.

"Am I that predictable?"

"Nah, I've still got a tracker on your phone."

I shake my head. "One time I go on vacation and you never let me turn it off after."

"Hey, that's what friends are for," she retorts, grabbing the pool stick and breaking.

Finally looking around, I see it's crowded for a Wednesday night. "Why's this place hopping?"

"No idea. I was going to ask Jim, but he isn't at the bar tonight," Delilah says, drinking her beer.

We know most of the guys who work here, but there's a new one behind the counter tonight. Lincoln's is normally pretty chill, and it's nice for winding down after work. I love clubs, and I love to dance. I don't get to do it as much as I used to, now that I work so much, but crowds don't bother me. Most weekdays, however, I stay away from clubs and stick to the dive bars.

We order food and play pool for an hour until Delilah wants to call it a night. The place is packed now, and I have to admit that my curiosity is piqued. Before I can find out why, Delilah pulls me out into the night and waves us down a cab.

By the time the cab drops me off and I make it into my apartment, I've pushed all thoughts of it aside. I barely have enough time to strip off my clothes before I've fallen face first into my bed.

Chapter Two

Royce

"Next we'll visit the head of security and you'll meet Pandora Justice. She runs the department, and I'm sure she'll help you with any questions you have," Henry Osbourne says as he leads me from his conference room to the elevator.

We've been in meetings for the past week, going over what he sees as the future of the company and where he thinks there's the greatest need for my expertise. I've met with board members and heads of every branch to try to supply him with the data he needs.

Henry has a great head for business, and the company is his first priority. It's unusual for someone around thirty to be driven by something other than money. But from what I've been able to assess, we both have very similar backgrounds. This was his father's company, and he's taken over. Now he wants to see it thrive under his control.

I've enjoyed working with him and discussing ideas for a better future. We've got a plan laid out, and now it's on to smaller department changes that could benefit everyone above and below in staffing.

Almost everyone I met came to the boardroom, but this time we're going directly to the security floor. It's different from what I've seen this week, but I'm curious to see the it.

"Is there a boardroom in security we can use?" Better to start with a question and see where that gets me. We step onto the elevator, and Henry hits the button.

He straightens his dark blue suit and brushes his hair out of his face. "Pandora likes things her way," he says, and lets out a sigh.

That's definitely not the answer I was expecting. It surprises me that he goes from confident and assured to almost nervous as the elevator doors open and we step off.

I follow him as he walks down a short hallway and into a large open area. There are desks all around and computer screens everywhere. People are talking to one another, and there's an energy around the room that's not quite excitement, but close. People say hello to Henry as we walk across the expanse, and he greets them all by name. I can tell this man loves his company but also cares about his employees.

The department takes up one floor, and that space has been opened up so information can be easily shared. It's definitely not made for privacy, but in a security department, there's no room for that.

There's an office on the far side of the room that's raised up a little. At least, I think it's an office. One wall is made of glass and the double doors are currently wide open. Closing them could offer sound privacy, but with the way it's situated, there's no way the person behind the computer could blink without someone knowing it.

Henry is as tall as I am, at six two, and so I can't see past him to who's in the office. What I do see is when his shoulders stiffen as he gets to the doors and knocks.

"Hey, Panny, I stopped by to introduce you to the consultant. Remember?"

"I told you about calling me that at work, Casanova," an unseen woman retorts.

He sighs and steps aside, holding out his hand. "Royce Davenport, I'd like to introduce you to Pandora Justice, head of security at Osbourne Corporation."

I look over and see a small woman bent over a computer and not even looking up at us. I want to laugh at her balls. She clearly doesn't give a fuck. I have to bite my bottom lip as Henry clears his throat to get her attention.

"Almost finished." Her hands click over her keyboard at a crazy speed, and after about thirty seconds, she stops and stands up. "If you could get me more people in here who can code, instead of idiot rent-a-cops who passed a two-hour course on mall safety, my floor would function a hell of a lot better."

Henry rubs his eyes and then looks at Pandora with pleading eyes. "Pan—"

"It's nice to meet you, Mrs. Justice," I say, holding out my hand, wanting to find out if she's married.

"Pandora. Mrs. Justice is my mom."

She takes it without hesitation, and I feel her firm grip meet mine. She's not trying to hurt me, and it doesn't feel exaggerated. Her hand feels strong in mine. This isn't a show where she's trying to seem tough. She actually is. I expected it to be soft and delicate, but her grasp feels like that of an athlete. The strength in her arm and her stance tells me that she's not afraid of me. Or anything.

It's a small touch, and I've sized her up with all my assumptions in one basket. And yet somehow I know I've got her all wrong. She's showing me who she is, but I have no clue where to begin. I've never met a woman so overwhelming. I'm drowning in her, and for a moment my head swims.

"If you need to sit down, there's a chair. I don't want you to fall over and bleed on my desk," she says as she pulls her hand from mine.

I'm sorry, but did she not just feel the earth stop moving?

I clear my throat and straighten my suit. My hair is cut short, and I can feel the cool air on the back of my neck just above my collar. I focus on that instead of the blood rushing to my ears.

"You'll have to excuse Royce. We've been in the boardroom all day. I promised him lunch, and I knew that was the only way I could get you out of your office," Henry says.

There's a low-lying threat to his statement, and for half a second I think Pandora is going to challenge it.

"Fine, Casanova. But I get to pick the appetizers."

They stare at one another, and for a moment I can picture them as children having this same discussion. Something green and angry rises in my chest at the banter these two have. Their inside jokes are irritating me and I feel excluded.

"Maybe I could have lunch one-on-one with Mrs.—" She snaps back to me with her deep blue eyes, and I correct myself. "Pandora. I think we've gone over enough for today, Henry. I can email you the rest of what we discussed, and I can handle the remainder here."

There's relief in his eyes as he smiles and shakes my hand. "Perfect. I'll speak to you tomorrow," he says, and nearly bolts out of the office before Pandora can protest.

"It's hard to respect your boss when you saw him poop his pants when he was six." She shrugs and grabs the bag hanging on the back of her chair. "Never work with family."

The warning somehow makes the green-eyed monster in my chest calm down, and I finally have a better understanding of the situation.

"I didn't realize you were related," I say, following closely behind her.

"Most people here know. It's hard for them not to since our parents all worked together, and we grew up basically like brother and sister."

Her long dark red hair is pulled into a tight ponytail, and it swishes back and forth as she walks. Her petite frame is moving fast, and I have to speed up my steps to keep up with her. I also have to force myself not to stare at her round ass when we get on the elevator. She pushes the button for the lobby and puts her hands on her hips.

"How do you feel about tacos?" she asks without looking at me.

"Never met one I didn't like," I say with a smile.

She slowly turns her head to me, and there's not a trace of humor on her face. When the elevator doors open, she slides on her sunglasses. "Watch yourself, Royce," she says before she steps off, and I have to hurry to keep up.

Fucking hell. I think I'm in love.

Chapter Three

Pandora

"I can smell the grease from here," Royce says, looking up at the Taco Hut.

I love this place and love it even more when it's nice out. They have little outside tables, too, so patrons can enjoy the sunshine. It's nice to get out of the office sometimes and get some sun. I haven't been doing that much lately. I really need a pool day with my sister.

I look over at him. He's once again standing too close, and it's really starting to annoy me, mostly because he keeps brushing up against me, and I don't like it. Not even a little.

It's amazing how easily I can lie to myself.

"You say that like it's a bad thing." I go to open the door, but he beats me to it.

He flashes me that perfect smile and brushes up against me again. I hate how short I am. Even in my heels, I still have to look up at him. I walk past, and the smell of tacos fills the air. But then all I can smell is him as he stands too close. He smells woodsy, nothing at all like I would have thought. With that suit that molds to his body so perfectly and a five-million-dollar smile, I was sure he'd have on some pungent, overpowering cologne. In fact, I think the smell coming off him is just the way he smells. Something about him isn't adding up for me. I can't put my finger on it, but it's there. Maybe it's the things he's making me feel, and I don't know how to explain it.

He leans down, and I turn my head, not willing to step back. "You don't know much about personal space, do you?"

That stupid smile only gets bigger. I shake my head, thankful for my sunglasses still perched on my face, because I didn't want him to see the childish eye roll I just gave him.

I walk up to the counter. "It's been a while," Sam says, coming back from the kitchen.

"I know, I know." I lean on the counter. "Miss me?"

"Every damn day." I see a shadow loom over me, and Royce has his hands folded over his chest.

His smile is gone now, and he looks pissed. I ignore him and go back to talking to Sam. Sam has owned the Taco Hut for as long as I can remember. My mom and dad would bring us up here a lot after school when we were kids. Then Penelope and I started coming on our own. We even studied for some of our finals in here while devouring late-night snacks. Sam always gave us homemade churros that were to die for.

"Don't mind him," I say when I see Sam eyeing Royce. "He doesn't know about boundaries. But I just met him today, so he could just be an asshole."

Sam smirks but gives Royce a glare. I hear Royce grunt something, but I don't catch it.

"How am I going to stay in business if your taco addiction is fading?" Sam teases.

"Blame Henry. He's the one working me to death."

Sam shakes his head. "Haven't seen him for a few months either."

"Because he knows I love this place and he's avoiding me right now. Do you have any fresh churros?" I ask, giving him my best smile. I want something sweet for later when I'm at work tonight and have nothing to eat. Tacos don't hold well, but the sugary dessert will.

"I think I may have a few," Sam says, his eyes softening. "Only for you, though." He shoots a look at Royce.

"Perfect, and I'll take my usual," I add.

"All right, eight tacos with extra cheese and sour cream."

I hear Royce cough and mutter, "Eight?"

I look at him and shrug. "They aren't giant. Kinda like mini tacos. They fry the shells, too, so they're crispy little heaven-sent morsels of pleasure." I can't stop the moan that escapes me when I talk about them. God, it's been too long.

"If they can make you make that sound, I'll take eight, too," he says, his smile back in place.

I turn in the other direction. I don't want to face him because I can feel my cheeks burn. That did not just happen. "I'll have a Diet Coke, too, and he's buying."

Sam chuckles and heads back to the kitchen. I go find a table outside and sit down. Royce follows me, setting my Coke down in front of me while taking a sip of his water.

"So I think our department is being staffed wrong. It's not that I need more people, I just think that maybe there's a faster way we can be doing things, something I'm not seeing. More productive, but not as much work—"

"Have you lived in New York long?" he asks, cutting me off.

I take a sip of my soda but ignore his question. "A few years back, a guy by the name of Jordan Chen used to work for us. Crazy good with computers, but he's retired. Anyway, long story short, we never replaced him. He had contingencies in place, but I think things have become dated and some stuff has changed."

"I can tell you were born and raised here. You talk fast."

I take my sunglasses off and study him for a second. "What's wrong? Can't keep up?" I raise an eyebrow at him.

He only smiles. Again. Then takes a sip of his water. I inhale slowly and try to stay on track.

"Anyway." I shift back as Sam comes over and sets our tacos down. "Thanks," I tell him as he walks away. "I don't think he'll want to do it. I mean, I can reach out to him, but he has a daughter. She's like him." I think about it for a moment. "Kinda like him."

"Did you know your lip lifts in the corner a little when you get annoyed?" His eyes are on my mouth.

"If you know you're annoying me, then why do you keep doing it?"

He shrugs and opens the box with his tacos, but doesn't move to eat one.

"Echo is—"

"See, your lip did it again. Does she annoy you?" He leans in a little, propping his elbows on the table and studying me. I don't like it. He's known me two seconds and already he's reading me like he's been doing it his whole life.

"Like I said, Echo is like her dad, but with some quirks. She can be—"

"Annoying?" he finishes. His eyebrows rise to let me know I did the lip thing again, but all I can think about is him watching my mouth now.

I take a breath and sit back, crossing my arms. Echo can be more than annoying. She has to control most things. "She can be unpredictable. If I tell her to do one thing and she thinks I'm wrong, she'll just do it her way. It's always her way."

"Then why would you want her?"

"Because she's normally right and five steps ahead. She's in her head a lot of the times and isn't always vocal. She just does it."

I knew this from experience. We shared a few classes together in school, and I got stuck on some projects with her. She'd actually skipped a few grades. Her parents are even pretty close with mine, so she was around a lot. But she normally favored hanging out with Penelope over me. She's damn smart. She's probably smarter than her father. They're always on the computer together, and I bet it would be easy for her to pick up where he left off.

"Are you in a relationship?" Royce asks, catching me off guard.

I was sure he was going to ask me more about Echo, but he doesn't really seem to care about work. All his questions are about me. That reminds me that I need to look into him, too. I did a soft check on him when Henry mentioned him, but I trust Henry. He wouldn't bring him on if he didn't think it was for the best. I always trust Henry's instincts because they're always spot on. Plus, the Davenport name is known around town. Royce comes from old family money. Probably thinks he can do and say anything he wants. I've met a lot of men like him. It's why, when I first meet new men I'll be working with, I'm firm so they don't think they can get something over on me.

Leaning over, I reach out and shut Royce's taco box. I pick it up and place his box on top of my box, then stack my churros on top of that.

"You just lost your tacos," I tell him.

I pick up my sunglasses, slide them back onto my face, and then grab the food. He can track me down when he actually wants to talk about work.

He chuckles as I walk away. Then I'm almost sure I hear something about it not being the tacos that he's after.

Chapter Four

Royce

"You sure you're up for this tonight?" Ezra asks from the couch.

"Leave him alone. Rolly's got this. Right?" Donovan gives me a worried look, but I shake both of them off.

"If I didn't know better, I'd say you two were starting to get soft on me."

"Pffft. After seeing that sweet little redhead you were talking to today, I've been nothing but hard," Ezra chimes in and winks at me.

I throw the remote at his head before he sees it coming, hitting him right between the eyes.

"Dude!" he shouts, and rubs the spot where it connected. "I'm sorry, okay? Don't mess up the moneymaker." He takes out his phone and looks into the camera to inspect the damage.

I'd caught Pandora today in the lobby. She's been avoiding me for the past few days, and I haven't been able to corner her in her office. From what I've heard she's usually at her desk, but lately she's been giving me the slip. I knew something was up the last time I was there to see her and they told me she'd gone to the ladies' room. I waited in her office for two hours and she never came back. Either she has some serious issues, or she was waiting me out. Lucky for her, I'm hardheaded and don't give up that easy.

She's been responding to all my emails, even if it's just a one-word answer. I've kept the messages professional and haven't stepped a toe out of line helping her the best I can with solving some of the problems she's been having. And I think she's right about hiring this Echo women. I've gone over some of her stuff and she's impressive. I even thought of reaching out to her myself so Pandora didn't have to because she seems to get annoyed with her would help. I came up with a plan for Echo to just do spot projects and not fully be on staff. More of a contractor for projects. She'd be more controllable that way. Giving her one task and program at a time then she is done until you need another done. She'd already come up with some amazing ideas that I knew would cut the work load down for Pandora. But somehow I think that's made her even more skittish.

Today she'd been in the lobby talking to the security guard at the entrance. Ezra and Donovan were there with me meeting Henry to go over the last of the proposal. My job at Osbourne Corporation is ending soon, and I don't know how many more opportunities I'll have to visit Pandora's office. When I saw her in the lobby, I had to take a chance.

She was wearing all black, and her eyes were rimmed with that dark charcoal, making her deep blue eyes pop.

I ached to take her long hair down from its tight knot and dive into it with both hands. To smudge the soft lipstick on her lips and make her react to me. I can't keep this bottled up much longer.

I walked over and tried to say hello but only got her cold shoulder. I'm happy to take anything from her, though, hot or cold. She doesn't seem to realize the more she plays hard to get, the more I want her. Although if she threw herself at me, I'd still want her pretty goddamn bad, too. I guess that makes me an even bigger idiot.

It took everything I had to let her walk away without crawling on my knees after her. I've never had this reaction to a woman before, and it's unnerving. I need tonight, if for nothing but to help settle my mind.

Once I got home and jerked off to the image of her lips saying my name while I was deep inside her pussy, I was able to get my thoughts together and send her the last of my ideas for restructuring her department and streamlining her data like she asked. About an hour after I sent it, I got an email back. It was only the word *thanks*, with her email signature below, but I knew that meant something big. She's not the type of woman to give things easily, and if she even took a second to respond, I knew she liked what I had to say.

I've always been a supporter of the *don't shit where you eat* policy. I keep it one hundred percent professional with all my clients, but something about Pandora is different. When she looks at me, there's heat there. If I knew she wasn't attracted to me, then I wouldn't come after her so hard. But I caught a hint of something I can't name, and I intend to find out what it is.

"That big German fucker is moving up," Donovan says, taking a beer out of my fridge and joining Ezra in the living room. "You sure you want in?"

"You know if you guys get pom-poms you could be my own personal cheerleaders." I grab a beer myself and lean against the counter. I pull out my phone and text the number I was given and ask for the location.

The three of us all got our own places a couple of years ago after we started making good money. I bought a loft in the Meatpacking District and have been fixing it up. It's still a work in progress, but I like doing it all with my own hands, so I don't mind. The kitchen and living space are done, and so are my bedroom and master bathroom. The spare rooms and baths are pretty much just bare bones, but the exposed brick makes it seem trendy instead of like a construction zone. There's a nice patio outside, but I've yet to tackle the jungle out there. Both my thumbs are black, so I'm leaving that for the last possible second.

Although they have their own homes, too, Ezra and Donovan always end up in my living room. I think it's because I have the biggest television, or maybe because I actually go to the store and buy beer. Either is a success in our book.

"I love wearing short skirts as much as the next guy, but we wouldn't be your friends if we didn't at least make sure your head is in the right space."

"I'm good," I say, looking at the two of them. They nod, knowing if I wasn't I'd speak up.

That's usually the case, at least. But I don't know if I'm in the same head space right now. Tonight I want to get my hands dirty. I can't shake my thoughts of Pandora, and it's driving me crazy. Every other second I'm wondering what she's doing and who she's with.

I was able to find out through subtle hints to Henry that she isn't married. I don't know if she has a boyfriend, but fuck him if she does. That's just a bump along the trail, and I'm all too willing to step on a man if it gets me closer to her. And that's the problem. I'm so consumed with my need for her that I'm willing to break up a relationship to get it.

I tip the bottle back and drain the rest of my beer. When my phone buzzes I check the text and see the name of the place on the screen. I slam it down a little too hard when I'm finished and grab my bag and keys.

"Where to?" Ezra asks, as he and Donovan get up and grab their stuff.

"Lincoln's."

Chapter Five

Pandora

"Got you!" my sister, Penelope, screams as she hops out in front of me.

I'm leaving work, and she thought she could sneak up on me. I saw her peeking through the glass door as I was walking out. It's hard to miss someone who looks exactly like you. Well, except for the little pregnant belly and her green eyes. Oh, and let's not forget she always has a giant Russian standing near her.

"Don't hop, *krasota*," her husband, Ivan, says, standing a few feet behind her.

Penelope rolls her eyes as her hand goes to her belly. She rubs it in such a sweet, mothering way.

"What are you doing?" I ask, like I don't know the answer. She knows something is up with me. It's like some weird twin thing we share. It's always been there, and it always will be. But sometimes I'd like a little emotional privacy from her.

"Well, what I'm *not* doing is giving you these." She holds up a white bag like she has victory in her hands.

I narrow my eyes at her. "Are those what I think they are?"

For a second I contemplate snatching the bag from her, but she turns, tossing the bag to Ivan, who easily catches it. Stupid twin thingy.

"Don't even think about it." She narrows her eyes back at me, giving me the exact look I gave her. I know those are her famous homemade brownies that we all fight over at family dinners.

"And I made them with real butter," she adds.

"What else would you make it with?" I crack a smile. Like she'd use anything but the full fat.

"I don't know. It sounded like a scary thing to add." Now I can't help but laugh.

"You're a dork." I walk over and pull her into a hug.

"Something weird is going on with you. I can feel it. Even in our texts you seem off," she whispers in my ear. I debate what to say to her, because I have been a little on edge.

"If I give you the truth, will you not ask me a million questions right now? I have some stuff to get done, and I have plans tonight."

"Fine," she grumbles. Pulling back, I place my hand on her belly. She's having a gender reveal party this weekend for the family. They haven't told anyone.

"Boy," she mouths to me, and winks.

"Same," I mumble, and her eyes go wide then stare down at my stomach. "No, not that. I mean men. This guy's... Grrr. Never mind. This weekend we'll talk," I tell her.

"Promise?" She studies me.

"Of course." I lean in, giving her a kiss on her cheek. Penelope can get everyone to do anything she wants. We always say she's our family's heart. Love just pours from her. She and her husband seem like opposites, but it works for them. He's a giant Russian who doesn't talk much and grunts when Penelope gets too far from him. Pretty sure he even has a tracker on her, and not some low-key cell phone one.

"Ivan." I nod toward him. He walks over and hands me the bag.

"Your mission over, *krasota*?" Ivan asks her. She gives him a nod and a wink. "Good. I wish to take you home."

"You always want to take me home," she laughs.

"*Da*," he agrees, like he doesn't know why she's giving that a voice. Everyone knows this. But truth is, Penelope is a homebody.

"Love you guys. Kiss my nieces," I tell them before bending down and kissing her belly. "Love you, too, little man."

I give my sister one more hug before they head off. I smile as I watch them go. I should have known she was going to pop up on me today after she randomly sent me the devil face emoji three times. I finish running a few errands before heading back to my office for a little while. I have a few hours to kill before I meet up with Delilah for some much-needed beers at Lincoln's.

I throw myself into work, trying to stay focused. But like it's been doing for the past few annoying days, my mind bounces back to Royce. I click my emails to see if he sent me anything in the last few hours but don't see anything. Annoyance once again creeps up my spine. And now I'm pissed at myself.

"What is wrong with me?" I mumble. I think that's the problem. I don't even know the answer to that question. For some reason, I'm annoyed that Royce didn't chase me the other day after I'd walked away from him. I wanted to be as far away from him as possible, yet I was disappointed when he wasn't there.

Then when he sends me emails, which I'm always checking, I get this stupid weird feeling in the pit of my stomach. It's frustrating not being able to control my reaction to him. To top it off, I know I'm being childish by avoiding him. I should be trying to work with him more. Help ease how busy I am at work, but here I am, being immature, which is something I've never done in my life when it comes to work. Though he seems to be solving a lot of my problems here at work without a lot of my help. Which only makes me think about him even more and all he's doing for me. He's going above and beyond and I'm acting like a brat.

Something about Royce isn't sitting right with me. It's like I'm missing something about him. I thought a few times about digging into him but changed my mind. I knew I wanted it for personal reasons, and I was *not* turning into some stalker like so many of my family members.

Dropping my head in my hands, I groan. I release a deep breath and look up at my computer to see that it's time for me to meet up with Delilah. I pick up my phone from my desk and slip it into the back pocket of my slacks.

Reaching into the top drawer of my desk, I pull out some lipstick and put it on before heading out toward Lincoln's. When I get there, I'm once again surprised to see it's so busy.

I see Delilah sitting at a table in the back, two beers in front of her and a couple plates of food. I walk over, take my blazer off, and sit on the chair.

"Hey," I say. She barely notices me as she looks around the bar.

"Hey," she replies with a small nod.

I reach down and pick up my beer, taking a few big pulls from it and enjoying the cold burn.

"Something's going on downstairs," she finally says, looking over at me.

"Really?" I glance to the back door and watch as people file in and out. In fact, the crowd has slowly gotten smaller as more people slip down there.

"Yeah, but no one is talking about what it is. I've had my ears open, but nothing." She looks over at me, pulling her eyes from the door. One eyebrow rises, and I know what she wants to do.

"Can I at least finish my beer and shove a few nachos in my mouth?" I ask her.

"That will take you two seconds," she laughs. I shrug and shove some nachos in my mouth before polishing off my beer. I stand with her and throw a few twenties on the table.

We make our way toward the door, and I wonder if anyone is going to stop us, but they don't. I walk down the stairs first. They lead down to a dark, narrow hallway, but I can hear noise coming from somewhere below. That's when light floods the space at the back of the room. The noise gets louder, and people are chanting. The place is dirty and smells like sweat.

"What the fuck?" Delilah mumbles behind me. When we get to the bottom, I realize what they are chanting.

"Rol-ly!"

"Rol-ly!"

"Rol-ly!"

"Holy shit, it's fight club," Delilah whispers excitedly. "It's underground shit."

A makeshift ring sits in the middle of the concrete room, with people standing all around it.

"Yeah," I agree as I look past the crowd, trying to see.

My eyes go to the ring where two men are already going at it. The once facing me looks like he's taken a few punches as blood runs down his nose. He isn't going to last another hit. He wobbles on his feet with his arms still up. His barrel chest rises and falls as he breathes hard, in and out. The crowd in front of me is making it hard to see, but Delilah and I push forward, both of us captivated by what's happening.

The one with his back to us makes me pause my forward progress. Tattoos run along his muscled back and down both his giant arms. He's freaking ripped. The dark lines that look like dragon scales make their way below the waist of his shorts, and for half a second I wonder just how low the tattoo goes. A light sheen of sweat covers his whole body, and I can't pull my eyes away from him. He's still bouncing on his feet, as if he could go for hours. He looks like a machine, and I feel a pulse between my legs as I watch him move. He's a beast from behind, and I can almost feel the power rolling off him.

The crowd keep chanting. He does a little hop before he lands a left hook and takes the man down to the ground. The bleeding guy falls hard, and the crowd erupts around the two men.

"That was hot," Delilah exclaims from behind me.

I nod in agreement, and just as I'm about to open my mouth, the fighter turns around.

My stomach drops as my gaze locks with Royce's. His eyes widen for a fraction of a second, just before a cocky smile pulls at his lips. The ref, or whoever is calling the fight, comes over and raises one of his big meaty arms in the air. The crowd chants even louder, and I swear to God, Royce looks at me like he just won more than that fight. Like he just won the right to fuck me.

His eyes stay locked on mine, and I feel as if I'm frozen in place. I don't know what I'm supposed to do, because right now I'm more turned on than I have ever been in my entire life.

"God, he's so hot. Think he'll be in the bar upstairs when the fight's over?" I hear a woman next to me say.

Then a very foreign feeling hits me. I drop my eyes from Royce, turning to look at Delilah.

"Crap. I forgot I have something to take care of," I tell her. It's the only thing I can come up with off the top of my head.

"That's cool. I'm going to hang out down here and see if there are any more fights. This is kinda badass."

I nod and say bye over my shoulder as I duck through the crowd. I take off, trying to get away from Royce once again. Why is it every time I'm near him, I feel like running away?

I almost make it to the stairs when a hand grabs my arm, turning me around. I close my eyes and curse myself. I know exactly who I'm going to find when he turns me around, and my eyes open to once again meet his.

Chapter Six

Royce

"What's the rush, baby?" I say, and see the fire in her eyes.

"Don't you dare call me that," she hisses, and jerks her arm out of my hold.

She may be pissed I caught her, but I know she likes what she sees. I've only got on a pair of loose shorts that hang low on my hips, and right now she's eye-fucking my happy trail.

"You like what you see?" She snaps her eyes back up to mine, and I see her blush. Fuck, what I wouldn't give to see if she blushes all the way down to her tits.

"What are you doing here? Aren't you afraid someone is going to smack that smile off your face?"

I smile even bigger, feeling my dimples crease. "No way, baby. I don't ever let them touch me."

"Must be a new experience then. Seems you've got people ready to climb all over you," she says, crossing her arms and looking around at the women watching us.

Goddamn, I love when she sasses me. "The only one I want on my jungle gym keeps avoiding me."

She lets out a huff and shakes her head. "I don't know what you mean."

"You know damn well what I mean," I say, taking a step forward. She takes a step back, trying to keep her distance. "But we're not in the office right now, baby. This is open territory. In fact," I say, taking another step toward her as she takes another one back, "I'd say it's pretty damn clear you're in my world now."

Her back hits the wall, and I move in front of her, putting my arms on either side of her shoulders. I lean down a little so we're eye to eye. I can see the pulse beating in her neck, and I want to lean forward and lick her there.

"This is my bar. Not my fault you were down in the basement. I just wanted to see what all the fuss was about."

"And?" I say, giving up the fight and leaning into her. I put my lips next to her ear and whisper, "Did you like what you saw?" I run my tongue along the edge of her ear and feel her shiver. "Because I damn well liked having your eyes on me."

"Royce," she says, and there's a catch in her voice.

"Fuck. Keep saying my name like that and it will get you fucked in the middle of that ring." I move my lips down her neck and feel her hands go to my chest. "Or is that what you want?"

Her fingers trail down my hard abs and to the edge of my shorts.

"I've gotta say I don't really like the thought of everyone in here seeing you take my cock, but it makes me hard as a rock picturing you under me and getting off."

"Oh God."

I move my mouth up to her lips and look her in the eyes. "I know you want to be in charge, but trust me, baby, it's better when you let me."

With that, I press my lips to hers, and it's like gasoline on a match. Whatever it is we've been dancing around finally comes to a stop, and we attack each other.

Her tongue pushes into my mouth, and I moan at the taste of her. In the next second I've got her picked up and pinned against the wall as I grind my cock against her.

"Put those fucking legs around me," I growl, and she does as I command.

Her thighs tighten as my hand goes to her shirt and slides underneath. I've got one hand gripping her ass as the other finds the cup of her bra and yanks it down. Her hard nipple is between my fingers, and I pinch the little bud as she moans. Her lower half rocks against me, and I've never felt anything like her. She's petite in my arms, but God, is she fierce. She's giving it back just as good as I'm giving it to her, and I feel the need roll off of her.

"I wonder if I can get a turn when she's done with him," I hear someone say from behind us.

Pandora breaks the kiss and glares over my shoulder. "Move along. Sloppy seconds aren't on the menu tonight."

I smile at her, and as if she's realized she just made a claim to me, a wall falls down in front of her and lands right between us. The woman behind me must leave, but I don't turn around to check. The only woman I'm interested in is in my arms, but even now I can see her pulling away.

"I need to go," she says, and drops her legs from around me, pushing my hand out from under her shirt. She takes a step away from me, but it might as well be a mile.

"Hey," I say, and she snaps her eyes back up to mine. I take her chin in my hand and lean down again so we are eye level. "Don't do that. Don't you push me away when you feel this, too."

"The only thing I feel is stupid for letting you embarrass me like this." She jerks her chin out of my hold and looks around the room.

"I've had enough of your bullshit, Pandora. Stop lying to me, and stop lying to yourself. You don't give a shit about anyone in here, so don't tell me I embarrassed you." I pull her into my arms, and she gasps. "You liked it, and I fucking loved it. You were meant to be in my arms. And the sooner you let yourself be okay with that, the better."

I kiss her hard, and she bites my lip. For half a second I think she's going to fight me, but instead she melts just like she did before. I could let this keep going, and we could end up just how we were a moment ago. But she needs to get her head together first.

I break our kiss and let her go, taking a step back from her. It's one of the hardest things I've ever had to do, but I can't stand her pushing me away again.

"I want you, plain and simple. And not just for a fast fuck in the ring. You feel this." I point between the two of us. "When you finally decide to take a chance, I'll be waiting."

Turning, I spot Donovan nearby, and he tosses me my shirt. I pull it on and give Pandora one last glance before I grab my bag from Ezra and make my way up the stairs.

I'm pissed off and could use another fight to take the edge off. I don't want to leave. I don't want to walk away from her. But chasing her isn't the way to win her heart. She's hardheaded, and if that's the way it has to be, that's fine, I'll wait. She's worth anything I'd have to do to get her.

I can only hope that she picks up the gauntlet I just laid down.

Chapter Seven

Pandora

I lie with Penelope in our childhood bed at our parents' house. Well, in Penny's childhood bed. It might as well have been mine, too. We shared rooms when we were little, but when we hit our teens, Mom and Dad gave us each our own room. But every night I would still find myself slipping into her room and into her bed.

I rest my hand on her belly. She was up here taking a nap with Ivan, but when I slipped in he smiled at me and left us alone. It was like any other Sunday with the family. Lots of laughter, lying by the pool, and more food than anyone could eat. But I didn't even feel like I was here for most of it. My head was far from here. I've been in another place, and it's filled with Royce.

"Hey," Penny says, her eyes fluttering open.

"Hey." Her hand comes to rest over mine on her belly, our fingers locking.

"You ready to talk about it?" she asks.

"There's this guy." That's all I get out before she has a giant smile on her face. "He's driving me crazy." She raises her eyebrows at me, and I let out a sigh. "Okay, maybe I'm driving him crazy, too."

"He must be something if he's got you all twisted. I've never seen you worked up over a man." She smiles. "Unless he was hitting on me."

I can't help but laugh. Penny and I used to give the boys hell in high school. They all followed her around like lost puppies.

"He bugged me when I first met him. Or I guess my attraction to him bugged me." I hated how much I liked the way he smelled. I hated how it made me feel when he got in my personal space. The way he kept asking questions about me.

"Why?"

"I don't know. I guess because I thought he was just another rich guy in a suit—someone Henry hired. I was taken aback by the attraction. He just went for it, but not in a way I was used to." I've never felt this way about someone, and I don't know if this is what I want.

"How so?" She studies me.

"He was aggressive, but not. Well, not at first. I knew he wanted me, but he didn't ask me out or anything. I kept trying to give him the cold shoulder, but he would still try to talk to me."

Penelope is full-on smiling now.

"What?"

She gives a little shrug.

"What? Tell me."

"He can tell you're like a skittish cat. You've got claws like Mom does, and he's slowly trying to move close to you. He's trying not to spook you too much, but he keeps coming."

I shake my head while a lump forms in my throat. "He stopped coming," I admit, and watch her eyes go soft. Then they harden and narrow. "What's his name?"

I can't help but laugh at the sound she makes. "You really should have your husband teach you how to growl better."

"Hey, I can still kick some ass. Don't let the belly fool you."

"There's more," I confess, and then proceed to tell her everything about the night at the bar.

"That doesn't mean he's done chasing." Penny glares at me. "He wants you."

"I guess, but still, it's been days, and the only time he talks to me is when he has to. I mean, I've run into him, like, five times a day, and nothing. He stares at me with those eyes I can't get out of my head."

"Does he work on your freaking floor or something?"

"No. Why?"

"Because that building is so big that no one is running into each other five times a day. Not unless they work in the lobby or on the same floor."

I think about what she's saying, and I suspect she might be right. "He's running into me on purpose," I say, and the realization makes me smile.

"Yep. He's trying to get you to finally admit you want him. He's giving you chance after chance to make your move."

I let her words sink in, and I bite my lip, thinking

it over. Why does the idea of him softly stalking me make me happy?

"Oh my God, you're blushing."

"Shut up," I scoff.

"Why are you running, Pan? You're not a runner. In fact, if I remember right, you're a secret cuddlebug."

"I am not a cuddler," I lie. I had every intention of coming in here to cuddle with her.

"Who do you think you're talking to? I slept with you for more than half your life." She gives me a look like I'm crazy.

"You're different. You're my twin."

She shakes her head at me. "I love you, so I'm giving it to you straight." Her face goes serious, and reminds me of Dad. "You're running because you're scared of a challenge that you might fail. That you could get hurt."

"That's not true," I say, cutting in. "Look at where I've gotten in life. I worked hard for this."

"I never said you don't work hard. You always have. The problem is, you know you're going to win. It's why when things might have been hard, you pushed because you knew you could do it. You knew you wouldn't fail because it was all on you. Nobody pushes like you do, Pan. You're a warrior, and we all know it. Anyone in a room with you for a few minutes knows that."

Her words start sinking in.

"You love on us, your family, because you know we love you. There's no failure in us loving you back. You let us have the soft side that no one else sees because we are safe." She reaches out, cupping my face. "This guy isn't safe, because you don't know what he'll do with your heart. When I thought Ivan didn't want me, I was a mess. You remember?"

I nod. I do remember seeing her in pieces. I also remember thinking I'd never let that happen to me.

"Love is scary, Pan. It's hard and unpredictable. But I can tell you it's worth every second. Step up to the challenge. I know you, and I know you want it. Go and get it."

Her words rain down on me. "You're right. Fuck."

Her hand drops from my face. "Pan, I meant like right now. Why are you still sitting here?"

I laugh and pull her into a hug. "Okay." I jump off the bed. "I love you," I tell her, going for the door.

"Love you, too."

I'm not shocked when I open the door and see Ivan standing there with a smile on his face. I smile back and head to the backyard to say my goodbyes. When I get to my car, I see Henry, in a suit, leaning against it. Only he would wear a suit to the family barbecue.

"Not avoiding me anymore?" I raise an eyebrow at him.

"Not now. It used to be Penelope we had to do this with."

I tilt my head, unsure about what he's talking about.

"Why is Royce Davenport asking me for your address?" His words make butterflies take flight in my stomach.

"When did he ask for it?" I try to play dumb, but the look on Henry's face tells me he isn't buying it.

"Called me about thirty minutes ago. He seemed pretty agitated. Then when I told him no he got pushy about it." He straightens and puts his hands in his pockets.

"What did you say?"

"I told him to fuck off. Like I'm going to give him your address. I should've seen it coming. He asks about you every damn day."

My cheeks warm at his words.

"Fuck me," Henry says, shaking his head. "Not you, too. Pandora, you know what happens when you fall in love in this family." He runs his hands through his hair just like his father does when he gets frustrated.

"Give me his address," I tell him, not caring. I want this.

"Come on, Pan." He gives me a look like I can't be for real.

"I'm not messing around. I want it." I pull out my phone and wait.

"Fucking hell." He rolls his eyes and lets out a sigh. "I'll text it to you. But only because I know you can take care of yourself."

He pulls out his phone and taps out a message. I see it pop up on mine, and I nod. He walks over to me and pulls me in for a hug.

"I know we've been at each other's throats the past few months with work, but I love you, and I just wanted to check in on this."

"I love you, too," I tell him. "But if I catch you leaning on my car again, we're going to have another problem."

He laughs, pulling away and walking into the house.

I hop in my car and put the address in my GPS. My hands are shaky, and I feel anxiety creep up my spine, but I've never been more sure of anything. I know I'm headed in the right direction.

Chapter Eight

Royce

I shouldn't have let her go.

That's the only thing running through my mind the past few days. I should have carried her out of that fucking basement and brought her home. I should have made her mine that second and not let any time pass between us.

I pace back and forth through my living room, trying to rack my brain about what to do. I've already been sneaking down to her floor for made-up reasons. I don't know how much more I can take. Days have gone by, and nothing. I see the look in her eyes. There's so much need there, and I know exactly how to make it better.

I clench my fists and grit my teeth. That damn stubborn woman is determined to drive me crazy. If she would just let herself feel what's between us, I know she'd see it. I know without a doubt that she'd fall into my arms.

Picking up my phone, I decide to call Henry again. Fuck everything. I don't care if this screws up working together or if it ruins my name. I won't let pride get in the way of what I want with Pandora. My finger hovers over the number just as I hear a knock on the door.

Looking up, I wait for Ezra or Donovan to walk in, but nothing happens. Thinking it must be a delivery from the doorman downstairs, I walk over and pull it open.

Standing in the doorway is my redheaded goddess. I'm stunned silent by her appearance, and I hold the door open with my jaw on the floor. Like an idiot.

Her hair is down, and she's looking up at me through her lashes. She's got on a black tank top and cutoff jean shorts and flip-flops. It's the most skin I've ever seen exposed on her, and my mouth begins to water. She looks casual, like she's been lounging around all day while I've been pacing like a maniac. I've never seen anything so beautiful in my life.

"Hey. Sorry to barge in on you, but I needed—"

Her words shake me out of my block of stone, and I reach for her, pulling her into my arms and kicking the door shut.

Before I know what's happening, I've got her pinned against the wall, and my lips are on hers. Fire ignites between us, stronger than our first kiss. I taste sweetness on her tongue and moan at the feel of her hands on my chest.

I grip her ass tight and grind her against the length of my cock. Every thick inch pulses for her, and I'm aching to be inside her tight, wet heat.

"Fuck," I moan as her hands move lower and I feel her fingers touch my stomach. "More." I hold her up against the wall with my lower half so my hands are free to pull my shirt off. "Touch me."

Her eyes are wide, and she licks her lips as her palms brush against my nipples.

"Did you come here because you want this?" I ask, watching her reaction. She nods, but I shake my head. "Not good enough." I run my hands up her thighs, feeling the warmth of her skin around my waist. "If you're here for a quick fuck, I'll put you on your feet and take your pretty ass home. But if you want what I want, then I need to hear you say it."

"Royce—"

"I don't want it to be like that, baby. But I won't play games with you. I'll wait, and it will fucking kill me, but I'll do it for you."

She runs her hand up to my neck, and I lean into her touch. I close my eyes and take a breath, wanting so desperately to have her.

"I'm here because I want it all. You, me, and whatever this could become."

I open my eyes and see the truth in hers.

"I've never felt this before, and I'm scared."

The raw vulnerability she's showing me right now makes my chest ache. It's exactly what I've been wanting her to say since the day I laid eyes on her. But I want her to be as sure as I am. Once I've had her, there's no going back.

"There's nothing to be afraid of, Pandora." I wrap my arms around her and look into her dark blue eyes. "I'll never hurt you, and I'll never leave you. So make sure when you tell me that you want this, that you damn well mean it. Because when you're mine, that's forever, baby."

"I'm trusting you with my heart," she says, and I smile.

"You've already got both hands wrapped around mine. Be careful with my precious cargo." I pull her away from the wall, and she laughs as I walk us back to my bedroom.

When I carry her in, I lay her down on the bed and lie on top of her. I'm not ready to kiss her yet, because I just want to look at her in my bed. I've pictured her more times than I can count, and none of the images did it justice.

"I've never done this before," she whispers, and I see her cheeks turn pink.

I could make a joke and lighten the mood, but I don't want to. This is important to me, and I want it to be important to her.

"Then I'll be gentle." I rub my nose against hers.

"I'm on the pill." She shrugs, and then opens her mouth to say something else, and I place my fingers on her lips.

"I'm clean, you're clean. No condoms." I wait a beat, and she nods.

When I take my finger away, I replace it with my lips. The kiss is soft at first, but when her hands get on my skin, I'm like an animal that's found its mate.

Reaching for the hem of her tank top, I pull it up and over her head, throwing it to the ground. Her breasts are bared to me, her pink nipples tight with desire. I suck one into my mouth as I slip my hand down the front of her jean shorts and into her panties.

Her warm honey greets my fingers as I spread her folds and pet her clit. She moans my name, and her hips rise as I rub little circles inside her shorts. I look down and see my hand disappearing below the waistband, and I feel pulse in my cock. Fuck, I want in there so bad, but I have to go slow.

Slowly, I push two fingers into her tight opening, rubbing her clit with my palm. I ache to rip her shorts and panties off, but somehow watching it like this is so fucking hot. I suck her other nipple in my mouth when I feel her body tighten around my digits. She's tight, but relaxes as I love her delicate body. I pet her as I would a kitten, gently and with ease. She responds in kind, moving her hand between us and rubbing the bulge in the front of my shorts.

The feel of her hand on me there is too much, and before I can control myself, I'm in motion.

Chapter Nine

Pandora

Suddenly my shorts and panties are gone and I'm left naked in the middle of Royce's bed. Heat and desire have pooled between my legs like never before, and I want him so much I may combust with need.

I watch with anticipation as he stands up to kick off his shorts and climbs back on the bed only wearing his boxer briefs.

"Wait," I say, holding out my hands. "Take those off, too."

He gives me that cocky smile that I love but also want to smack off his face. But he does as I ask as he reaches in his underwear to fist his cock and then slides them off his body. Fuck, could this guy be any sexier?

"Spread those thighs, baby. I've waited long enough to get a taste of heaven."

I throw my hands over my face to hide the blush. I'm never shy about anything but right now I can feel my whole body blushing. I feel my legs being jerked open and his mouth biting the inside of my thigh.

"Eyes on me, Pandora. I want to see you fall in love."

The bastard winks at me, and just before I can reach out to smack him, his face ducks between my legs and I feel his mouth on my center.

"Oh Jesus," I groan as the delicious sensation flows up my core and through my veins.

"Royce will do just fine, baby. No need to call me anything else."

I want to growl. I want to kick at him for being such an arrogant asshole. But the things his tongue is doing to me have made me lose all thought.

He slides his hands under my ass and lifts me up to him. My legs go over his lower back, and my bottom half is completely off the bed. He's right, though. I watch him with such focus that I can't possibly look away, and I might actually be falling for him at the same time.

No one has ever made me feel this good, and I don't just mean between my legs. My heart is full as I run my fingers through his hair, and he tells me how beautiful I am, how good I taste. Passion floods every cell in my body as he seduces me with endless praise on just how perfect I am for him.

If I had known it would be like this, I would have sat on his face the second he walked into my office.

Reaching up, I rub my breasts and play with my nipples as he looks up from my sex. His eyes narrow, and he moans in agonizing pleasure as he enjoys the view. I'm teasing him and I'm temping his control, but I'm so close to orgasm that I can't stop myself.

He knows I'm close, too, because every time my

breath hitches and I'm at the peak, he pulls me back in. He's edging me, keeping me on the cusp, and I'm insane with want.

"You going to beg for it?" he asks as he kisses the inside of my thigh and runs his nose against my clit.

"Never," I say, and I damn well mean it.

"That's my girl," he whispers, and winks at me.

Goddamn him for making me fall even harder for him.

I open my mouth to protest, but before I can get a word out, Royce has flipped me over on my hands and knees and is pulling my back to his front.

His arms come around my waist, and I feel the large length of his cock resting between my legs. He's sitting back on his feet and brings me onto his lap, with my legs on either side of his.

"I want you like this the first time. This way you can control it."

His big hands run up my stomach. One cups my breast and the other slides back down to my pussy. I feel his rough digits gently stroke my sensitive clit, and my orgasm is barreling down on me again. My body is wound so tight he's playing me like a guitar.

"Slide down real easy, baby." He kisses my shoulder, and I feel him nuzzle my neck. "I want to make slow, sweet love to you."

He's handed me the keys and told me to drive. I didn't expect this from him. I thought he'd get on top and it would be something I'd have to grit my teeth to get through the first time. But like Royce, he's never what I think.

The head of his cock presses against my entrance, and I feel the girth of him. But his hands roam my body, and his kisses trail up and down my neck, and I relax. I breathe through the pinch of pain and slowly lower myself onto him. I can feel the slight tremble in his touch as I take more and more of his length until I'm fully seated.

There's nothing in the world that can explain just how good it feels to take him into my body. I can't describe the fullness not only between my legs but in my heart as I hear Royce's voice in my ear. I expected it to hurt, and I never expected it to feel this good.

"So perfect. So beautiful," he whispers, and pets my clit.

"I'm so close," I breathe, already on the edge of pleasure.

My body is locked tight around his, and I feel his lips at my ear. "Slow, baby. Real slow."

I rise up, and his length drags out of me, letting me feel every hard ridge. The head of his cock rubs some perfect place inside me, and I cry out when he hits it.

"Now let's focus on that. Right there," he says, rocking back and forth in short bursts right against that secret place inside me.

The feeling is torture of the sweetest kind, and it's like I'm being branded from the inside out.

"Royce. Oh shit." I grab his arms and dig my nails into his skin. Somewhere in the back of my mind I hear him encouraging it, telling me to mark him.

The slow, steady thrusts right on that one spot have

my eyes closing tight and sweat breaking out all over my body.

"I'm going to come right there." He thrusts against it, and I cry out.

My body shakes, and I scream as the orgasm ignites in my blood and sends pleasure to every inch of my body. My fingers and toes feel like they're on fire, and I nearly collapse onto the bed.

But Royce holds me tight, and I feel heat between my legs as his seed spills inside me. The two of us combined spread on the insides of my thighs, and I can feel every pulse of his cock as he gives me more.

His orgasm triggers another wave of pleasure between my legs, and his fingers slow their steady thrum. My gasps of breath have slowed down, and my heartbeat is beginning to return to normal.

His lips kiss my shoulder, and I can feel him smile against me. "Mine," he says, and hugs his arms around my body.

A wave of exhaustion hits me as he lays me down on the bed and spoons in beside me. There's a blanket pulled over us, and his strong arms keep me safe. I've never felt more at peace in my life, and I snuggle against him.

"Get some sleep, baby. You're going to need it."

Chapter Ten

Pandora

Kisses rain down my spine and slowly wake me. I look over my shoulder to see Royce's lips lingering in places before he moves to the next spot. This is the second time he's woken me up with his mouth. The first was with him between my legs. He ate me until I came and I fell asleep again.

"We gotta go, baby," he says against my skin, but makes no room to move.

"Hmm," I mumble, wanting to fall back on the pillow, but I like watching him kiss me.

"I don't want to move from this bed," I admit. I glance over to the window and see that the sun has already set.

"I have a fight tonight," he says before he gives me a long lick up my spine. "I feel like I've been waiting to get you in my bed since forever."

His words make me smile. "We've known each other maybe two weeks," I tease, rolling over.

He comes down on top of me, his big body blanketing mine. I reach up and run my finger along his lips. He smiles at me. That perfect smile that always drives me crazy. I lean up and kiss his dimple.

"I thought it would take me months to turn you into a cuddler," he says. It's then I notice that I wrapped my arms and legs around him. I'm pretty sure I slept on top of him, too, for most our nap.

I want to say something smartass about it, but I just hold tighter to him and bury my face in his neck. I want this. I don't know why I've been fighting it. It feels good to be wrapped around it. It feels like where I belong.

Before I know what's happening, we're moving. I hear the twist of knobs, then warm water hits my body. I pull back to look at Royce. He takes my mouth in a soft kiss before placing me on my feet.

"You really have a fight tonight?" I'm torn between wanting to see him in action again and wanting to crawl on top of his naked body.

"Yeah," he says, putting soap on his hands and rubbing my body to clean me. It's so natural and intimate. For some reason, jealousy shoots through me at the thought of him doing this with someone else. "What's the face for, babe?"

"Nothing," I lie, not wanting to tell him what I'm thinking.

He leans down and places a kiss below my ear. "Don't do that. Don't put those walls up," he says.

"Do you have a lot of women in here?" I finally bring myself to say. I want to do this, and I know if I do, I need to be open, say what I'm thinking and not hide or act like I don't care when I really do.

That smile spreads on his face. "I'll smack you," I tell him.

I raise my eyebrows at him, but then his face grows serious. He leans down, cupping my face in his big hands.

"No," he says simply, and I can see the truth on his face. "I've never been serious with someone before. For a while I thought something might be wrong with me. I didn't have an interest in women, or even men, for that matter. I felt nothing. But then you walked into my life, and I knew. I just hadn't found my woman yet. I found the one who challenges me and makes me feel things I've never felt."

I lean up and kiss him. It's slow and soft, and before I know it, I'm in his arms, wrapping myself around him again. I'm lost when his lips touch mine, and it's like drowning in a pool of love. I've never experienced anything so safe and free.

It takes us thirty minutes to finally pull ourselves from the shower, and when we do, my fingers and toes are wrinkled like raisins.

"You're not wearing that," Royce says.

I glance over at him. He's dressed in dark jeans and a tight gray shirt that molds to his body. He's got a gym bag slung over his shoulder, and he's glaring at me.

"Well, this is all I've got, unless you want to run by my place," I say, walking toward him. "Besides, I wear whatever I want." I walk right past him and don't stop as I walk out the front door. I know he's going to follow me, because I feel him behind me. I didn't have much choice in what to wear, but I can't say I don't like poking the bear.

I have my jean shorts on and one of Royce's white undershirts. My black bra is easily seen through the white material. Luckily I had some boots in my car, because I wasn't going to wear flip-flops to a bar fight. Or whatever this is called. This isn't something I would normally wear, but I'll tough it out. I'm showing off more skin than I want to, but it will be fine. Plus, when I saw Royce's eyes heat up as he looked me over, it only solidified my view on this outfit. I like it even more now that I know how he feels about it.

"I have a feeling I'm going to be fighting more than my opponent tonight," I hear Royce say from behind me. A little squeak leaves me when I'm lifted up and thrown over his shoulder. He slaps me on the ass before putting me back on my feet. I glare up at him, but he only leans down, kissing me and ignoring my stare.

His hand cups my ass. "Come on, baby. We gotta get going." I pretend to be mad as I walk around his car. He opens the door for me, and I slip in. He reaches in and buckles my seat belt. I want to tell him I can take care of myself, that I know how to put my own seat belt on. But something about him taking care of me, just like in the shower, gives me a warm feeling in my stomach.

He slides in the driver seat and we take off toward the bar. "Do you get nervous before a fight?" I ask, because he seems completely calm. I would at least be a little jittery.

"Nope," he says easily. "Been doing it awhile now."

"Your face seems too pretty to fight all the time," I tell him, earning me that cocky smile of his.

"I'll try and keep it that way tonight. Wouldn't want

my woman thinking I'm not the best-looking guy in the room."

I roll my eyes at his comment.

When we finally make it to the bar, I start getting excited. Everyone seems to know who Royce is. He keeps a possessive arm wrapped around me as we make our way through the crowd. It's weird having a man hold on to me and stake his claim, but I like it. I know I can take care of myself, but it's nice having his protective body telling everyone in here I'm his.

"You know you'll have to let me go so you can get in the ring, right?" I look up at him. For once his face doesn't have that smile. No, now he looks a little irritated.

"Yo, Rolly, who's the girl?"

Royce's arm tightens around me even more. I glance over to the man who called his name.

"She's none of your fucking business. That's who she is," he throws back. The other man is big. He looks like he spends ten hours a day in a gym. I wouldn't be shocked if someone said he was on steroids, but Royce doesn't seem to care. "If I were you I'd watch myself. No point poking me before we get in that ring. Don't make it worse for yourself."

Jesus, he's going to fight this guy? He looks like the after picture in a bodybuilder commercial, but Royce doesn't seem to care.

"Never seen you on a girl before. Got me wondering."

I look around and see other people are looking at us, too.

I go to say something, but Royce drops his arm from around me. "You need to go somewhere else."

"Damn, that pussy must be good if it's got you all riled up. How about we bet on her own little ass? Whoever wins the fight tonight gets her," he challenges.

Now I'm fucking pissed. I try to step forward, but Royce beats me to it. His arm shoots out, and he swings. His fist meets the guy's jaw, and there's an audible crunch throughout the room. Before I can even blink, he's throwing his other fist and connecting with the other side of his face. The man sways back, and Royce thrusts an uppercut, sending him down hard to the concrete floor.

Everyone starts cheering and yelling Royce's name. I stand there a little shocked, but the crowd is going nuts.

Royce comes back to me, wrapping his arm around my back.

"Guess the fight is over," I murmur through a smile.

Something about him getting jealous and possessive makes the warm feeling come back to my stomach. I never thought I would have something like this, or even want it. Now I'm starting to see why Penny loves it when Ivan gets all territorial. It makes you feel special.

"Told you not to wear that outfit." He shakes his head, but I just keep on smiling as his hand moves down and squeezes my ass.

Chapter Eleven

Royce

I growl when I feel her press her lower half against my cock. She knows exactly what she's doing with that ass of hers.

"You trying to get fucked down here tonight?" I ask, looking in those dark blue eyes.

"Maybe." She bites her bottom lip, and I swear to God I wrap tighter around her pinky.

"I bet you didn't know you were such a dirty girl."

"Yo, Rolly!" I look up and see my boys coming down the steps.

Ezra looks at the ring behind me and shakes his head. Donovan just laughs and looks at me with a questioning expression. "Guess there's no fight tonight?"

"No," I say, and don't elaborate.

"Someone went caveman," Pandora says, and waves to the two of them.

"I don't blame him," Ezra says. "You're coming down to the lion's den dressed like that. I'm surprised another fight hasn't broken out."

"Not yet," I say, narrowing my eyes on her. "And stop looking at her," I snap at Ezra.

"Hey, just looking out for my man's girl." He winks at her, and I feel my fists clench.

"Since you're here, and there's no fight, how about we get a beer and see what shakes out? I bet they'll stack another one. It's early." Donovan looks past me and then back to us.

My grip on Pandora's ass tightens, but she has other ideas.

"Sounds like fun. The first one was over way too soon." She blows me a kiss as she wiggles out of my grip and goes to the bar.

"Goddamn that woman," I say to myself, but Donovan slaps me on the back.

"Cheer up, Rolly. You've only got another sixty years or so of it to deal with."

The thought of spending the rest of my life with Pandora warms the place in my chest that I didn't think was alive until I met her. Donovan and Ezra know the type of guy I am. They know that I don't take things lightly when it comes to women. If I've put my claim on Pandora, they know it's for keeps. She's the one, and I'm done. It's that simple for me, and they know it. Now let's see if Pandora can get on the same page as them.

Pandora grabs a stool and orders us beers. I go over and pick her up, then sit down and put her on my lap. She wiggles on top of me like she's annoyed, but when her ass finds my cock, her eyes grow wide. I lean into her hair and put my lips against her ear.

"Keep wiggling like that and I'll bend you over this

bar." I take her lobe between my teeth, and I feel her shiver. "I'd have to murder everyone in this room for watching you get fucked. But I'll always give you what you need."

I slide my hands up her bare thigh until I get to the edge of her short shorts. They show just the edge of her cheek and barely cover her pussy.

"Royce," she breathes, and I shake my head.

"Call me Rolly when we're down here. It makes me so fucking hard to think about you cheering my name while you watch me." I play with the edge of her shorts, running my fingertips where the denim is frayed. "If I get in there tonight, I'm gonna fight. And when I'm done, I'm gonna need to fuck. So if I step in that ring, you better be wet and ready for me, baby."

"That middleweight from Boston is here tonight. You want in on that?" Donovan asks, breaking our moment.

I look up at him and then to Pandora, raising my eyebrow in a question. She licks her lips, and I see a blush creep across her cheeks as she nods.

"Yeah, I'm fighting," I say to Donovan.

"All right. I'll set it up," he says, and disappears through the crowd.

I drink my beer, and Pandora watches me, eyes locked on my mouth and then on my throat when I swallow. Her body is so hot, and I can see the change in her breathing, see her hard nipples poking against the thin white shirt.

"You stay beside Ezra until it's finished," I say. It's not a question, but she nods. "And you stay where I can see you. Right up front."

"It's done," Donovan says, coming back over. "You're up in ten."

"Let's go change," I say, getting off the stool and pulling Pandora behind me.

I take her into the bathroom and lock the door. I push her up against it and lift her, letting her legs wrap around my waist.

"Tell you what, baby. However many seconds it takes me to knock that guy out is how many hours I'm going to spend between your legs when we get home."

"Is that a threat?" she asks smugly.

"You saw me KO that guy in about a second. You sure you want me to go that quick?" I give her my cocky smile that I know makes her wet, and I'm not disappointed when she rubs her lower half against me.

"Take your time," she says, but then she becomes serious. "Be careful, okay?"

"You just take care of what's most important to me, and I'll do the rest." I kiss her softly and then drop her to her feet so I can change.

When I've got on my loose shorts and no shirt, she looks me over like I'm a piece of meat and she's a vegan who just fell off the wagon.

"You keep giving me eyes like that and I'll have to fuck you right now."

There's a loud pounding on the door. "You're up, Rolly."

"Promises, promises," Pandora says, and runs her hand across my chest. "Put your shirt on right after. I don't like other women seeing you without it on."

I reach into my bag and pull it out, slipping it back

on over my head. She looks at me with shock on her face, and I wink. "For your eyes only."

We walk out and make our way over to the ring. I stand at the edge, and Ezra is right there beside Pandora, waiting on her.

I lean down, giving her a kiss and laying my claim in front of everyone. I want to deepen it, but I force myself to stop and then move my lips to her ear. "Count for me, baby."

Stepping away, I walk in the ring and look over to her thighs squeezed together. My job is almost done. Now I just need to knock this guy out so I can go take care of my woman.

The bell rings, and I step up, my fists held in front of my face. The guy comes at me, and I block his first few punches, dancing around the ring. I hear the crowd cheering, but over all of it I hear Pandora say my name.

The primal beast inside me grows ten sizes, and I smile at the man across the ring from me. He doesn't stand a chance.

Stepping forward, I lay a one-two punch on him and then another. That's all it takes to make him go down. He's a big guy, but I've got my woman shouting my name, and I'd never let her see me fail.

He's not knocked out, so the ref has to come over to count it out. I turn to see Pandora with one hand on her throat in surprise as she watches me. It was fast, but the time is ticking. I count out loud with the ref, giving her my dirty smile. Knowing I'm going to love every minute I'm between those smooth thighs of hers.

"Three, two, one," I say, stalking toward her. But before I make it to her, she's leaping into my arms.

I carry her through the crowd, and her mouth goes to my neck, licking and sucking on me.

"Get out of my way," I growl at people who are blocking us.

When I get to the bathroom, I kick it closed and shoot the bolt.

"Goddamn, that was hot," she breathes right before my mouth connects with hers.

I set her on her feet and unbutton her shorts, pushing them off her hips along with her panties. I lift her back up and press her to the wall as I pull my rock-hard cock out.

"Seven seconds," she moans right before I thrust all the way into her tight pussy.

"Seven hours of heaven," I say, pulling back and thrusting back in.

"Royce!" She cries out, and I do it again.

I ride her hard, needing the release from tonight. The adrenaline has built up from the fighting and thinking about all the men out there checking out what's mine.

"Right now, you're getting a quick fuck. I'll take my time when we get home." I reach between us and rub her clit. "This is fast and dirty. But I know you like it."

I feel her tighten around me as I pound her against the wall. I strum her sweet little nub, and she moans, burying her mouth against my chest.

My cock aches to come, but I feel how close she is. I grit my teeth and hold off, wanting us to go together.

The punishing rhythm is enough, though, and I don't have to wait long.

"That's it!" she cries, tensing up and biting my chest as she comes.

"Fuck," I moan, and empty into her, feeling my whole body shake from the intensity of it.

Her body goes limp in my arms as I feel the heat of our passion coat her thighs. I'm going to have fun cleaning that up later.

"God, you're so hot when you fight," she says, smiling at me with heavy eyes.

"Not as hot as you are when you're on my cock." I flash her the smile I know drives her crazy, and she rolls her eyes, smacking my chest playfully. "I'm going to take you home, feed you, and then make good on my promise."

"You're going to get lockjaw," she says, kissing my lips. "But then I won't have to hear your cocky comments."

"I'll take that trade-off."

Chapter Twelve

Pandora

"I've never seen you look nervous before," Royce says, looking over at me.

It's been over a week of pure bliss with him. I even said "fuck it" and called out of work for two days just to stay in bed with him. I'd been working my ass off, and I figured I'd earned it.

He's right, though. I hardly ever get nervous. "I want them to like you," I tell him, looking up at my parents' house.

Penelope has been begging me all week to bring Royce to the family dinner. While I want to, I'm a little reluctant. Not because I'm embarrassed to bring a guy around, but because I want everyone to love him.

Royce reaches over, sliding his hand into mine. "Baby, I promise everything will be fine." He gives me a little squeeze.

"My family is close," I tell him, trying to make sure he understands how important this is to me. I don't want him to think I don't want them to meet each other. I just want this to be perfect.

We're more than close. My family is everything to me. I actually think that's part of the reason why I never went out and found—or wanted—a boyfriend. I had people close to me at home and didn't think I needed it anywhere else. Plus, I always thought I'd never find someone as good as my dad. I wasn't willing to settle. I saw how he treated my mom, and I thought that was rare. I didn't think I would ever find a love like that. My mom's strong-willed like I am, but he handles her, while letting her be who she is. I'm a leader like her, and most men are threatened by that. Royce seems to get off on it, though. It's probably why I love him.

I freeze for a second, processing the thought that just popped into my head. *I love him.*

"Then I want to be close to them, too," he says, breaking through my internal shock.

"I'm different with them," I admit. "It's not like the 'work me' most people see."

"Baby," he sighs. God, I love it when he calls me that. I used to think guys calling their women that was annoying. Maybe I was secretly missing something, because when Royce says it, I melt into a puddle. "I've spent a week worshiping your body and feeding you. I know there are two sides to you. I love them both."

"You love them both," I repeat, only really catching one word.

He grabs me, pulling me onto his lap and positioning me so I'm straddling him. He takes my mouth in a deep kiss that has me worked up in seconds.

"Loved you from the moment I saw you," he tells me. He runs his hand up to my hair, pulling my ponytail. "I felt it that first time you took my hand."

I'd felt it, too, but it scared me. "You make a different part of me come out. With you, I feel like I don't have to have any walls. I can just be me," I admit, because it's true.

"I'm like a fucking king because you're that way with me." He rubs the back of my neck before pulling me to him and taking my mouth again. This time I deepen it, wanting to fall into him.

I pull him closer, but suddenly the car door is flying open.

"Oh. My. Fucking. God," I hear Penelope say.

"Royce, this is my sister," I mutter, pulling back from the kiss and blushing because I got caught making out.

"He's hot," Penelope says. I hear Ivan growl and look over to see him moving her behind his big body and away from us. "Not hotter than you." She rolls her eyes. "Get out of the car," she says, before yelling, "Mom, Pan is making out in the car!"

Now it's my turn to roll my eyes. Royce chuckles as I climb off him and out of the car. The smile on Penelope's face is giant. Ivan has his arms around her, cupping her belly like her baby might pop out at any moment and he might need to catch him.

"She's mine," Ivan says simply, his eyes boring into Royce. I know Royce can fight, but I'm not sure anyone wants to come up against Ivan when it comes to my sister.

Royce wraps one arm around me, pulling me into him. "And she's mine," he says simply.

They glare at one another, and Ivan nods to me. "And she's my sister. Hurt her and I promise you it will be the last thing you do."

It takes me a little by surprise, but his words make me smile. Ivan and I have become somewhat close over the years, with him being married to Penelope, but I didn't think he'd say that.

"And this is my brother, Ivan," I say, smiling.

"Hurting her is the last thing I'll ever do," Royce says, pulling me even closer to him. Ivan studies him for a moment before nodding.

"Look at them. He's all cuddling her and she's letting him!" Penelope says excitedly. She looks like she's about to burst into a pile of sparkles.

"Pan," Mom says. I turn to see her and Dad standing in the front door. Dad has his arms crossed over his chest and is giving Royce a death stare. Mom has a little smirk on her face. She and Penelope seem to be the only ones who are happy here.

"Hey," I say, waving to them.

"You going to introduce us?" Dad says.

"This is Pan's man," Penelope says before I can get a word in. "She needs a ring and a baby," she adds, and I feel myself blush. I give her a hard look, and she just shrugs.

Mom and Dad make their way out the front door. "Mom, Dad, this is Royce. We kinda work together," I tell them.

"This is what had you in knots last week?" Mom asks. I feel myself redden even more. I had no idea I was a blusher, but leave it to my family to pull it out of me.

Royce reaches out, taking Dad's hand. Dad holds it for a second before letting it go.

"I wasn't in knots," I say as Royce takes Mom's hand next. Mom just smiles more, looking just like Penelope.

"Don't let her lie to you," Royce says before kissing the top of my head.

"I know my girl. And I know you," Mom says as she lists off Royce's life history. She even knows a bit more than I do.

"Mom," I scold, but she shrugs.

Penelope keeps on smiling, and Dad stands there, seeming to know it all.

"We run one of the biggest security firms in the States. Do you think we don't know who you're dating?" Dad says.

Royce lets out a bark of laughter. "Well, I hope I meet your standards."

"Not that it matters," I add. "I'm keeping him."

Dad studies me for a second before a smile finally pulls at his lips. While I was a little nervous to introduce them to Royce, I knew they would be happy. My parents are so in love and want the same for me. Dad has even been poking me about when I might bring someone around.

Royce squeezes my hand, and I smile at him. "Okay, guys, now that's out of the way. We're leaving," I tell them.

I go around and give everyone a goodbye hug.

"You just got here," Penelope says grumpily in my ear.

"He just told me he loves me," I whisper back.

"Yep. They have to go," Penelope says loudly, making me shake my head.

My mom and dad try to protest, but Penelope goes about pushing them back into the house.

Royce looks at me with confusion and holds his arms out, palms up.

"Get in the car," I tell him, and he raises his eyebrows at me.

"You get in the car," he says back, and I roll my eyes.

I go around to the other side and get in and wait for him to slide into the driver's seat. Reaching over, he pulls on my seat belt for me and waits.

"Drive," I grit out.

"What has you all pissy?" he asks as he slides his key in then backs out of the driveway.

"The man I love just told me he loves me, and I haven't gotten to say it back."

We've only traveled a few yards when the car comes to a sudden halt as he hits the brakes and throws it into park.

Before I know it, my seat belt is off, and Royce yanks me out of my seat and onto his lap.

"Say it."

"You can't demand it," I tease.

"Baby..." His voice comes out rough and deep, with so much emotion in it. "Say it."

"I love you," I whisper for the first time to someone outside of my family.

He stares at me hard for half a second before his mouth hits mine. His tongue pushes in, and I kiss him back just as fiercely. I don't know why I ever fought this. His hands tangle in my hair, and all I can think is that this love is what I've been waiting on my whole life.

"We're getting married," he tells me as his lips move to my neck.

"You're bossy."

Normally I would get mad, but something about the way he's so assertive and sure of what he's saying does it for me. I feel myself smile and close my eyes, loving the feeling of his lips on me.

His grip on my hair tightens, and my pussy clenches. God, what this beast of a man does to me.

"Say you'll marry me," he pushes, and I moan at the strong grip he has on me.

He's tough, and it goes straight to my core. I'm not used to someone being so firm with me. I like it, and he smiles, knowing damn well I'm getting off on it.

"I'll marry you," I tell him, because it's what I want. It might be crazy fast, but I don't care. This man was made for me. "We could fly to Vegas tonight."

He smiles and then leans forward, giving me a soft, sweet kiss. It's the complete opposite of what we were just doing. Then he's putting me back in my seat and going back into my parents' driveway.

"What are you doing?" I ask, wondering what the hell is happening.

"I'm going to go ask your dad if I can marry you."

He's giving me that cocky grin with his deep dimples, and I melt. I once wanted to smack that look off his face, and now all I want to do is kiss it. He gets it. He understands what my family means to me.

"I love you," I tell him again.

"I love you, too," he says before getting out of the car and taking me with him.

Epilogue

Royce

Two years later

"What are you two in here doing?" I ask, seeing Pandora and our daughter, Lavender, playing.

"I'm teaching her how to throw a punch," Pandora says, holding up her hand for Lav to hit.

"Hey, I'm the fighter in this family. I should be the one doing it." I lean on the doorframe and cross my arms. The sight of the two of them together completes a piece of a puzzle I never knew I was building. We've talked about having another one, but Pandora says Penelope has enough for the whole family.

"Nah. I want her to be good at it." Pandora winks at me, and I growl, getting on the floor with the two of them and lying on my back while Lavender crawls on me.

We kept my loft in the city for Pandora to work a few days a week. I do most of my consulting from home now, so I'm mobile. We have our house on "the compound" as we love to call it, and stay out there the rest of the time.

I stopped fighting after Lavender was born. It's not that I didn't enjoy it, but having kids changed our perspective on things. Suddenly it wasn't just me and Pandora fucking in bathrooms in the basement of dingy bars. Although we still manage to do that on date night. I wanted to give our little girl the world, and that included my time, too. Once I made the decision to step out of the ring, I never looked back. Getting in the ring was a good time, but it's not a sport you can really work at long term, and I was ready for it to end.

But there's one thing that hasn't changed, and that's my love for Pandora. If anything, it's grown over the past two years to a level I can't even comprehend. I never knew love could be like this, and every day it grows stronger. Pandora's dad told me that it's that way for him and her mom, too. I see it when they're together, and that's what I want for us.

"Are you all packed up?" I ask, sitting up to kiss Pandora.

"Yep. It's nice having stuff at both places, though, so all we have to do is grab the essentials."

I reach out and grab her breast, and she giggles. "What? Just the essentials, right?"

"You play your cards right, and we can have a babysitter tonight."

"Your sister is having baby fever again," I say, picking up Lav and taking her over to the changing table.

"I know. She says one more, and Ivan agrees. But I

think that man would give her as many babies as her little body can carry."

She comes up behind me and wraps her arms around my waist, resting her cheek on my shoulder.

"If we timed it out right, you could both be pregnant at the same time," I say.

"Oh God! Can you imagine? Penelope would go nuts."

I blow a raspberry on Lav's belly and listen to her giggle. "Might not be so bad. She's already a year old. Maybe we should have them close together."

"Sounds like you're the one who has baby fever," she says, smacking my ass. "Are you and Penelope in cahoots?"

I hide my smile from her and try to shrug casually. I may have been talking to Penelope about cycles and when they would both be ovulating again. Ivan didn't like the talk at first, but as soon as Penelope was talking about being fertile, he was right there with us.

"Royce Davenport, turn around and look at me," Pandora demands.

I pick up Lav and hold her up beside my face. "Would we lie to you?"

Pandora bites her lip and shakes her head. "You're not allowed to use her cuteness to get out of trouble. Come to Mama, little one."

She takes Lavender, and then I scoop the both of them in my arms and walk toward the door.

"Tell you what, why don't we let your parents watch little Lav tonight, and you and me have some alone time? You know, see what happens."

Pandora rolls her eyes, but I know she's thinking about it.

"I can't say I don't like it when you try to knock me up," she says as I put her on her feet so she can grab her bag. I take it from her, and then take the baby, as Pandora locks up.

"Then just shut that pretty mouth of yours and let your man make things happen."

"I think your dad is trying to give you a brother or sister," Pandora says as she walks past us.

"I'm trying my best, baby girl," I whisper to her, and she giggles at me.

Epilogue

Pandora

Five years later

"Oh my God, Pan, that guy is totally checking you out," Penelope says from beside me.

I look up to see a guy at a bench in the park near us looking our way.

"Whatever," I say, blowing it off. I'm in yoga pants and a tank top, with what I'm sure are at least three different kid stains.

"Seriously. He keeps looking over here," she says, poking me in the ribs not so subtly.

"Dude," I say, to get her to stop. "Maybe he's checking *you* out."

I look over to see the kids playing together in the grass and lie back on the blanket to soak in the sun.

"Don't even play like that. Ivan is more than ten feet from me. If he hears you, he'll come over here and murder everyone," she says, looking around for him like she's excited by the possibility. "Besides, I'm, like, eleven months pregnant with my fifth kid. I think Ivan might be the only man alive who finds me sexy."

"Let's hope so. If he found out someone else did, we'd all be in trouble."

"I do love how possessive he can be." She sighs dreamily, and I roll my eyes.

I can't hate it, though. Possessive is one of my favorite features on my man. I lower my glasses and see Royce with our two little girls getting snow cones. His ass is looking way too good in those jeans today. Ivan is beside him, and he waves to Penelope, who blows him a kiss. God, I love her and how ridiculous she is sometimes.

"Oh shit. He's coming over here. What do we do? Should we throw something at him?" Penelope is freaking out, and I want to laugh and cover her mouth at the same time.

"Excuse me, but do I know you?" the tall, thin guy asks, looking down at me.

"No," I say, looking back to where Royce and Ivan are standing, but their backs are turned to us.

"They are not going to like this," Penelope mumbles in a singsong voice.

"Are you sure, you look very familiar. Have you been to the art gallery on 7th?"

"Nope," I say, sitting up now so the guy isn't looming over me so much.

"It's strange, because I own it, and I swear I've seen you at one of our exhibits."

"You've mistaken me for someone else. My hus—"

"My name is Drake," he says, interrupting me and kneeling down, holding out his hand.

Penelope leans past me and whispers to the stranger. "Look, Drake, you seem like a nice enough guy, so I'm going to save your life." She looks to our guys and then back to him. "Those men are straight killers. You need to walk away slowly and never look back."

He smiles like Penelope is being funny, but she pulls back and shakes her head. "Oh shit. Here we go."

I turn to see Royce stomping over to us, the snow cones gripped in his hands so tight all of the ice is falling off them as he gets closer. He's trying to hang on to them as the girls are hot on his heels reaching for them, and it's a pretty funny sight.

"Are you talking to my *wife*?" He says the last word like I belong to him and it should be obvious to the world.

I want to laugh at how comical it is, but I know if I do I'll only get him angrier. Nothing sets my Royce off like someone stepping between him and his ladies. That includes our daughters.

Royce hands the girls the snow cones, and Lavender complains that half of hers is on the ground, while Sam shrugs and drinks what's left in the cup.

"I'm sorry, baby. I'll get you another once I get rid of this asshole." Royce looks back to Drake, who's already standing up and backing away.

Just then Ivan walks up, and I bury my face in my hands, groaning.

"I tried to tell him," Penelope says in a smug voice, crossing her arms over her chest and shaking her head.

Ivan doesn't stop once he gets to us, though. Instead, he keeps stomping toward the guy. Drake's eyes widen with fear, and he backs away. Ivan keeps going, then Drake turns and runs. Ivan ends up chasing the guy out of the park and out of sight.

"God, I love him," Penelope sighs, watching Ivan walk back to her.

"Come with me," Royce says, pulling me from the blanket and taking me with him to the snow cone vendor. "Should have brought you the first time."

The girls sit down with their aunt and uncle and finish what little they have left of their icy treat.

"Don't get all grumpy," I tease, wrapping my arms around him and leaning close.

"I dropped my snow cone," he complains, and he sounds like a little boy. It's so adorable, I start laughing.

He growls and then turns, grabbing me up and squeezing my ass.

"You're lucky you're hot," I say, kissing his lips.

"Yeah, well, I'm cursed that my wife is so damn hot. Can't keep them off of you."

"Well, I did wear my best yoga pants," I say, and shrug.

"I told you your ass looked too good in them."

"Give me my smile," I say, and he does as I ask.

He beams at me, giving me that cocky-ass grin with dimples showing. I kiss each one before I kiss his lips, and he grinds against me.

"You get turned on when you get jealous," I mumble against his lips.

"I get turned on when I've got you in my arms. And you damn well know it."

"Maybe you should remind me," I push.

I'm not disappointed when he throws me over his shoulder and tells my sister and Ivan to take the girls home. He's got something he needs to take care of, and it has to do with my sassy mouth.

God, I love my man.

* * * * *

Acknowledgments

Thank you to Carina Press for loving our stories and not allowing us to leave this world. Our readers are grateful to everyone there, and so are we! Lots of love to our editor Angela James for knowing our voice and letting us roll around in this one on our own. Don't ever let it be said that you don't know how to herd cats!

To our friends…thank you for stealing us away on signing vacations to help keep us sane. To our husbands, thank you for putting up with our crabby attitudes, late-night writing sessions and forgetting to cook dinner. Again. You are the butter on our bread…and we mean the full-fat kind.

And to our readers. You guys begged for more, and we gave it to you. Although now we're terrified we've fed the beast and you won't take no for an answer. Thank you for your kind emails, social media messages and words of encouragement. It means so much to us that you're a part of our stories. We hope you love this book just as much as we love you.

DON'T GO

For Miles and Mallory...
We wouldn't have Henry without you.

Thank you for *everything*.

Prologue

Henry

I stand in the lunch line with my tray, trying not to get caught staring at her. There's an ache in my chest as I watch her in the kitchen dishing out food and bringing it over to the buffet. She shouldn't be serving all these spoiled assholes.

I know I come from money, but that's not what defines me. My parents taught me that it didn't matter the dollars I had in my pocket; all that mattered was what was in my heart. I never realized what they truly meant by that until the first time I saw her. When I laid eyes on her, it was the only time in my life that I cared about what someone thought of me. Of course, like any senior in high school, I wanted to impress her. But more than anything, I wanted her to see I was different. That I wasn't some spoiled rich kid who slid in here because of my last name. I wanted her to look at me and see someone kind and smart. Okay, and maybe supremely hot.

Kory Summers moved here at the beginning of our

senior year, but I don't know her story. She's quiet and keeps to herself, and I don't have many classes with her. I've avoided asking about her because I don't want to draw attention. It's clear she wants to remain under the radar. She's a scholarship student, which is obvious from her place on the other side of the counter during lunch.

Our high school is one of the best private schools in New York City, and if you can't afford to pay the astronomical tuition, they offer a few rare scholarships that require working for the school in exchange for an education. We call the kids in these programs "ships." The ships usually band together and don't mingle with the rest of us for the most part. It doesn't take a brain surgeon to figure out why, but Kory even stays clear of most of the ships unless it comes to work.

I've poked around and found out she hasn't joined any teams or clubs. She has no after-school activities other than helping some of the ships with the rowing equipment after practice. If I didn't pay so much attention to her every movement, if I was like every other person in this school, I might have missed her completely. But I don't miss a thing when it comes to her.

"Yo, Henry, grab me three of those," my cousin Pandora says as she walks past me and cuts in front of the line. I look down and see Kory place small plates of tacos in front of me, and I grab some for Pandora.

My twin cousins go here, too, but they're almost a year younger than me. Most of the time, we eat lunch together, unless Penelope is in love this week and she'll sit with whatever guy she's picked up.

By the time I look up, I see Kory's back as she walks away and could kick myself. It would have been a perfect opportunity to say something to her. Anything.

It's not that I'm shy or that I have a problem talking to girls. I just don't make the effort most of the time. My parents have ruined me for falling in love, and I don't know that I want to play the hook-up game like some of my guy friends.

My dad fell in love with my mom the second he saw her. He did insane things to make sure he'd have her and the two of them are inseparable. They're crazy about each other, and being a kid in the shadow of that makes it feel like finding what they have is impossible. So instead, I've gone out of my way to avoid the possibility of that kind of love and focused on school. Until Kory showed up. Now I can't get her off my mind.

"Are you going to move or what?" someone says from behind me, and I tear my eyes away from Kory to go to the cashier.

I pay for my food then spot Pandora. Penelope is talking to a table of cheerleaders, but she's still holding her tray in her hands, so I'm guessing she'll be over to our usual table soon enough.

A few minutes later, Pandora gets to our table. Though she already has a full tray, she reaches over to take her tacos without so much as a *thank-you*. I've long ago stopped being surprised by how much she can eat.

"You talk to her today?" Penelope chirps as she arrives and sits beside me.

I pretend I don't hear her and take a drink of my soda.

"You're becoming obvious," Pandora mumbles around a mouthful of food, and Penelope agrees with her.

"It's true. We only noticed it in the beginning because we know your tells. But now you're getting sloppy."

"My tells?" I ask, feeling defensive.

Pandora rolls her eyes and Penelope smiles as she folds her hands in front of her.

"Just a few things here and there. But don't worry, we'll only use this knowledge against you in poker." Penelope takes a drink and then raises an eyebrow. "So, are you asking her to prom or not? You didn't even go last year."

I shrug and glance back over to the kitchen. "She doesn't even know I'm alive," I mutter.

"Henry, I hate to break it to you, but with the exception of me and Penelope, you've got the vaginas well aware of your presence," Pandora says, leaning back in her chair and rubbing her stomach. "Just ask her. She'll say yes, and you can get over this weird phobia you've got of chicks."

"I don't have a phobia," I protest, but already I see the two of them give me identical eye rolls.

"You can call it what you want, but there's nothing wrong with being in love," Penelope says.

"Not all of us can find it every week like you do," Pandora pokes at her, and I fight a smile.

"I can't help it if you two aren't as romantic as I am." Penelope takes a bite of her fries and looks over to Kory, then back to me. "What's different about her?"

I shrug because I honestly don't know. I can't explain

why no girl before her ever made me turn my head, but this one has me spun in circles.

"I can't believe she dresses like that," Pandora says, and my eyes snap to hers. "Hey, don't look at me like that. You know I don't care. I'm just saying, it's kind of badass. I like that she doesn't give a fuck. She's got my vote."

"I'm not taking a vote on it," I say, but Penelope sits up straighter.

"She doesn't roll her uniform skirts up like most of the hoochies here, and she wears a hoodie almost every day. She's definitely not seeking attention. If anything, she's trying to disappear. You're a really nice guy, Henry. I think you'd be a good match. I vote yes, too."

"Uggghh," I groan, burying my face in my hands.

"She's got gym next period, but she hides out in the campus library. She has a doctor's note," Pandora says as she piles up her tray with trash and stands.

"Wait, how do you know that?" I reach out, grabbing for her arm, but she moves it too fast.

"I know everything." She's smug as she walks away, and Penelope just giggles.

"All right, I'm off to meet the prom committee. We've got lots to do before this weekend." Penelope leans forward on her elbows and looks into my eyes. "Don't let fear stop you, Henry. You owe it to yourself to see it through."

I remain silent as she leaves and don't move until the bell rings. When it does, I'm on my feet and headed in the direction of the library before my mind can do anything to stop me. I've listened to it for long enough. I'm going to see what my heart has to say.

The library is on the other end of our high school campus and it looks like it might as well be a cathedral for the size of it. The doors are gigantic, as well as the vaulted ceilings and stained-glass windows inside. There are about five floors below the first one, and while I've been inside plenty of times before, I have no idea where to even begin looking for her.

When I walk inside, there's an older lady at the front desk, scanning barcodes on the backs of books. The sign in front of her reads "Information," and it may be my only chance. When I walk up, she glances at me then back at her books.

"How can I help you?" she asks, not looking at me.

"I'm here to meet my study group, but I don't know where to meet them." The lie is so easy I surprise myself.

"Don't you know how to text? Even I do that."

"I would, but I didn't get her number." The librarian looks up at me over the tops of her glasses with a patronizing look. "She's short, blond hair, sweatshirt and glasses."

Something flashes in her eyes, then they narrow on me. "Three floors down. Back left corner," is all she says, and I move on before she can stop me.

I take the stairs, because I don't want to die in an elevator that looks like a death trap. When I go down three floors, it's freezing. The cool air, combined with being underground, turns this floor into an icebox. No wonder Kory is always in a hoodie.

The corner is blocked off by rows of books that go from floor to ceiling. There are hundreds in just this area, but I don't pay attention to them. I don't really have a plan for when I find her, I'm just going to wing it.

Walking past the rows, I make my way through the maze until I spot a table with four chairs in the back, with someone sitting at it. It's hard to tell if it's Kory because they've got their hood over their head.

I walk over and slide my book bag onto one of the chairs and pull out the one beside it. "This taken?" I ask, and watch as she looks up at me.

There's complete confusion on her face as she watches me. She even looks past me and then at my seat before pushing her hood back. Her dark green eyes meet mine, and the ache in my chest is back.

"Are you serious?" she asks, with a laugh in her voice.

"Yeah," I say, suddenly feeling stupid.

"There are about seven hundred desks in this library. About eighty on this floor alone. And you want to come all the way to the back corner and sit at the one table that's occupied?" She raises an eyebrow and leans back in her chair. For a split second, she reminds me of Pandora, but there's a vulnerability in her eyes. "No thanks, my table is full."

"You don't even know me," I say, feeling like she's brushing me off just for the sake of turning me down.

"Oh, but I do. You're Henry Osbourne, heir to the Osbourne fortune. You're captain of the soccer team, debate team and mathletes. You've got a 4.0 and a full ride to Yale waiting on you when you're ready. I know all I need to know about you, and I know that chair you want to sit in is taken. So either you move along or I will."

"That will make this much easier," I say, sitting down. "Now all you have to do is go with me to prom." Kory's mouth pops open, and all I can think about is how much I want to kiss her.

"You don't even know me," she says, repeating my words.

"You're Kory Summers, scholarship student. You don't like gym." I look around at the stack of books. "You must like reading." I pause, trying to think of something else, and just go for honesty. "And I think you're beautiful."

A blush hits her cheeks, but I can see she doesn't know what to do with the compliment. So instead of letting her sit there embarrassed, I move on.

"I don't know much about you, but I thought maybe you'd go out with me and I could find out." I shrug, feeling a little embarrassed, but a small smile pulls at her lips.

"And you thought our first date should be to the prom?" She shakes her head. "You realize it's this Saturday, right?"

"I thought waiting until the last possible second would give you less chance to back out."

She laughs at my lame joke and leans forward. "Or maybe give me less time to find a dress," she mumbles.

"So that's a yes?" I feel hope stir in my chest where the ache was. Can this be happening?

"From the rumors I've heard, you're a nice guy. I don't have any plans on Saturday." She tucks her hair behind her ear and pulls out her phone. "Give me your number and I'll text you mine.

"I can't believe I'm doing this," she murmurs to herself after she keys in my information.

"What, agreeing to go out with me?" I ask, pretending to be affronted.

She grabs her bag, stands up and walks around the table. She looks down at me, and her green eyes are filled with something I can't put my finger on. She opens her mouth to say something, but then she changes her mind. Just when I'm about to ask her, she says with heavy words, "Don't break my heart."

I never meant to.

Chapter One

Kory

Ten years later

"Mom, I'm fine, really."

I'm thankful the lie comes out easily. I'm not used to lying, especially to my mom. I normally tell her everything, but I don't want her to worry about me. I want her to have a good time on her vacation.

"It was just so fast. I thought you liked your job in Boston."

"I did. I mean, it was okay."

I'd taken the job at Bare Benefit right after I graduated from Harvard with a master's in chemistry. Heck, they had me lined up for the job before I even graduated.

I took it because the pay was good and I'd grown to love Boston over the years. Plus, I got a little obsessed with makeup in college. New York still held bad memories for me, and I'd barely been back since high school. I'd only come for big holidays and I'd spend my time holed up in my mom's house until I could leave again. I'd actually left high school before the school year ended. I tested out early, which was easy for me.

With such high scores in math, I had my pick of schools, and Harvard was still somewhat close to home. Even if I didn't want to go home, I liked knowing my mom was close and I could go back any moment if I wanted to.

"I got offered a job here in the city. It's a big raise and a promotion. They've been after me for a while." I've turned down Pure Lush four times over the past two years. Which is crazy. It was a phenomenal offer. But when they called me the other day, it was like fate was stepping in. It was perfect timing.

I still feel bad about not giving my old job two weeks' notice, but I had to get out of Boston as fast as I could.

"Oh, honey. I'm so happy you're back." My mom sniffles into the phone.

"We'll see if you think that when you come back from vacation. I don't know how long it's going to take me to find a place in the city."

"No rush," she says hurriedly. I know she'd let me stay forever if I wanted.

"It'll be easier for work if I live in the city. But I promise now that I'm back home we'll spend a lot more time together," I tell her, feeling a little guilty.

My mom lives at home alone. She's a nurse and keeps busy, but I know the feeling of living alone, too. The solitude gets old at times.

Right now she's off on a cruise in Alaska and won't be back for a few weeks, which I'm thankful for. I can't let her see me right now.

"You don't know how happy that makes me, honey." I feel guilt at her words.

Mom and I used to be so close when I was growing up. It was always the two of us. I know they say your mom shouldn't be your best friend, but it wasn't like I was some wild child.

If it hadn't been for my mom when I was a kid, I wouldn't have had any friends at all and would have lived inside one of the books I kept my face in most of the time. She's always been so supportive of me, even when I wanted to leave high school early. She knew I had to go, and she made sure that I could.

"I love you, Mom. Go have fun," I say in the happiest voice I can muster.

"I love you, too, honey," she says, and we say our goodbyes.

I set my phone down on my childhood bed. Nothing has changed. Everything is how it was when I was in high school. I walk over to the mirror over my dresser and look at my lip. There's a small crack in it, but some of the swelling has gone down. I lift up my shirt and look at the bruise on my ribs. They hurt way more than my lip, but a kick is a whole lot more punishing than a backhand to the face.

A tear slips free, and I wipe it away as fast as I can. I turn from the mirror and drop my shirt. I'm sick of crying. Sick of still being scared that Jason might come after me. He has to know I'm gone by now.

I did everything to cut off contact. I deleted old email accounts, left the city and even changed my phone number. But I know if he really wants to find me, he will.

All he has to do is pull my employee file. I know I have my mom's info as my in-case-of-emergency. I just can't recall if I volunteered her address, too. I think it was only her phone number, and she didn't say anything about getting a weird call. I would think she'd mention something like that.

Thinking about Jason makes a chill run up my spine and the need for a shower coat my skin. Heading toward the bathroom, I peel my clothes off and turn the water on as hot as I can stand it.

I've only ever dated once in my life. Well, I'm not even sure you can call it dating. Henry—my heart aches at the thought of him. It's been ten years and my heart still does a funny flutter when I think of him.

He hurt me in a different way than Jason did, though, not that I ever dated Jason. But the hurt Jason left on my body will fade.

I grab the soap and wash my body, being careful over my ribs and trying to avoid looking at the discoloration while I do it.

I'm still not sure exactly what happened with Jason. It was like a switch just flipped. He was the owner of the company, and I thought we were friends. That the attention he gave me, the raises and promotions were because he respected my work. I thought he wanted to hear what I had to say and that he valued my opinions.

I thought.

Over time, his touches began to linger. Lunch meetings turned into dinner meetings, and the talk went from work to personal. He started pushing wine on me, then stronger drinks. What I thought was two people becoming friends was something much more sinister.

I didn't have many friends, being as shy as I am. And it was even harder once I was promoted. I was head of my entire department, and no one wants to be friends with the boss.

Then one night Jason tried to kiss me. I pushed him away, shocked by the advance. Jason was married, and I'd even met his wife a few times. She seemed nice. I told him this wasn't right and that I thought we were just friends. I only ever wanted to be friends. But he didn't like what I had to say, and that's where it all went wrong.

"You're right, you're right, Kory. I don't know what I was thinking. Too much wine, and the wife and I are going through a hard time." He shakes his head in what looks like regret. *"Can I use your bathroom and I'll be on my way? We can pretend this never happened and just go back to how things were."*

I hesitate for a moment but then nod, sliding my key into my door and opening it. "First door on the right," I tell him, motioning down the hall. He shuts the front door. Before it even closes, the back of his hand strikes my face. The blow sends me to the floor.

Black spots dance in my vision. The taste of copper fills my mouth. Then a kick lands on my ribs, ripping the air from my lungs. Tears fill my eyes and leak down my face. "Jason!" I cry, still unable to believe this is happening. That he's doing this to me.

My eyes flutter open. He's leaning down over me. His face right in mine. "Don't be such a fucking tease, Kory," he says calmly, as if he isn't attacking me. Ev-

erything about him seems calm. It's like we're talking about the weather or something.

"I'm sorry," I force out. *I don't want him to hit me again. My lungs feel like they're on fire. A slow smile pulls at his lips. I suddenly feel like a mouse caught in a trap, with the cat ready to pounce at any moment.*

He grabs me, pulling me to my feet. My knees almost buckle, but he keeps me on my feet with his arm wrapped around me.

"Say my name again," *he barks at me, pulling me even tighter to him. I cry out his name in pain, the pressure he puts on my ribs almost too much to take.*

He smiles even bigger as the black dots dance in my vision once again. Then he's leaning down toward me, his intent to kiss me clear. Utter panic rolls through my body when I realize where this is going.

I cough and let the blood that filled my mouth spill out, coating my lips. He freezes, a look of disgust on his face. He releases me. I stumble back.

"I'm sorry," *I plead, trying to make it seem like an accident.* "I didn't mean to ruin our first kiss," *I lie.* "I've never done this before," *I add.*

"You're a virgin?" *he asks, sounding excited. I nod. He stands a little taller, puffing his chest out. A chill runs down my spine.*

"I don't want our first time to be like this," *I tell him, hoping that maybe I can calm him down. Get him out of here. Make him think I want this, too.* "I was a little shocked you even wanted me. I've wanted you for so long. I got scared you would change your mind if you knew I was a virgin."

He takes a step toward me. It takes everything in me not to retreat.

"Get yourself cleaned up." His phone rings, startling both of us. He pulls it out of his pocket. I stand there, unsure what to do. He listens for a moment. "I'll be home in a little bit, honey," he says, and I know it's his wife. The tone of his voice is so different than it was moments ago.

My heart pounds as I wonder what he's going to do to me. He ends the call and puts the phone back in his pocket.

He takes another step toward me, tucking my hair behind my ear. A tear slides down my cheek.

"Don't cry, sweetheart. She'll be out of the picture soon enough and it will be just you and me." My stomach rolls and I want to throw up. I try to keep from shaking. "I'll be back tomorrow and we'll do this right." He sounds so sincere, as if he hadn't beaten me only moments ago.

"Okay. I like that idea," I lie once again. His eyes go to my mouth. My bloodied mouth.

"Tomorrow you'll get your first everything." With that, he turns and leaves. I stand there for a moment before I rush over and lock the door behind him.

He's freaking crazy. I know I have to get out of here. I drop down on my sofa and let the tears fall for a moment.

Then I stand, knowing I need to put as much space as I can between me and this man, and I know where I want to go.

Home.

I turn off the shower, still not feeling like I washed Jason away. I can only hope he doesn't come looking for me.

Chapter Two

Henry

I sit back in my desk chair and look out at the city. It's the same window my father looked out of for longer than I can remember. I've been thinking about him and my mom a lot lately. They're off on another vacation enjoying one another and life. They call and check in, but I know they're happy traveling the world.

I've got a stack of papers on my desk that I need to go over, but I don't feel like it today. For some reason, I've felt an ache in my chest for the past couple of days, one I haven't felt in a long time, mostly because I've learned to ignore it. But the beating in my heart can't be ignored, and my thoughts drift to Kory, just like they always do.

I rub the place between my ribs and wonder if this is exactly what my father felt like, looking out onto a city where he knew the love of his life was, but she was just beyond his reach.

For years I tried to fight it, but it never once went away. Not even for a second.

I think back to the day I asked her to the prom and how it all seemed so perfect. I picked her up at her apartment and met her mom. We laughed and held hands while we went to my aunt and uncle's house for pictures. She looked so beautiful in her white dress. I kept thinking she looked more like a bride, and I loved it. At eighteen years old, I pictured her walking down an aisle to me, and I wanted so badly for it to be real.

But then everything went to shit, and in an instant, it was gone.

I'm my father's son, even though I've spent my life trying not to be. I knew the way he was with my mom. He was out of his mind for her, and nothing else mattered. I never wanted to be that way. I didn't want someone to have that much power over me because it was dangerous. That's what I knew to be true. But all it took was one look at Kory and all of that changed.

It's been years and I haven't gotten over her. The day she disappeared was the day I lost my soul. She took it with her, and I've never so much as glanced at another woman since. Why would I? I might have been young, and it might have not meant anything to her, but I've never felt anything like it since. I knew when I was eighteen that I'd met the love of my life, but she slipped through my fingers.

I could have tracked her down a thousand times over. I could have hired a team of men to find out where she was and drag her back to me, but that wasn't what she wanted. She left town two days after prom without a single word. I sent hundreds of texts. I called until my number was blocked. I even went to her house so many times that her mom called the cops. Kory chose to erase me from her memory and broke something inside me. I chose to give her the only thing I could, which was my absence. I knew some people thought we were just kids, but it was more to me than that. It still is. Only I choose to bury it deep down inside me and put food on top of it. Pandora always tells me food makes everything better. I hope one day she's right.

My parents knew something was wrong the next day, but I didn't tell them what happened. I was embarrassed, and even though it wasn't my fault, I felt responsible. Kory hated me after that night, and she wouldn't hear me out. I tried everything I could to explain, but eventually it wasn't about what I wanted. It was about giving her peace.

Now my life is all about my work and my family because I don't have any room for anything else. Kory Summers is the majority stakeholder in my heart, and that's never going to change. I've learned to live with the ache, but some days are easier than others.

There's a knock on my office door and I turn around to see my assistant, Joseph, coming in, holding his tablet with an expectant look on his face.

"The set of contracts I gave you this morning need to be sent to the courier by the end of business today. You've had three calls from our legal team over the new proposal from the Adams Group, but I've directed them to the right people instead of bothering you with them. I've canceled your lunch as per your request and I've moved your afternoon meeting to tomorrow at eleven," he says, touching the stylus to his screen. He looks up at me through horn-rimmed glassed with a polite smile.

"Thanks, Joseph, I appreciate it," I say, sighing and grabbing the stack of papers. I cleared out my afternoon so I could go through this, and I haven't even started.

"Is there anything else I can do to help you with the contracts?" he asks, patient and ready to work.

"No. At some point I'm going to have to rip the Band-Aid off," I say, opening up one file.

"Give us some privacy, kid," Pandora says, walking straight into my office and sitting down in the chair in front of my desk.

"Can I get you anything to drink or eat?" Joseph asks. He knows my cousin all too well.

"The usual," she says, and thanks him when he quickly brings her back a Coke with a tray of snacks.

I wait for Joseph to exit and close the doors to my office before I acknowledge Pandora's presence.

"Any particular reason you're barging into my office and being rude to my assistant?" I ask, happy for another distraction and a reason to avoid the tedious work I hate to do.

"She's back," she says, and lays a legal-size envelope on my desk.

"She who?" I reach over and pick it up, turning it over in my hands. It's blank on the outside, but it's heavy. "What is this?"

"It's Kory. She's back in the city. She moved here two weeks ago. At first, I thought maybe she was visiting her mom, but she's taken a job in Manhattan. You know her mom still lives in the same building on the Lower East Side. Crazy, right? Must be rent controlled."

"Stop," I order, holding up one hand and gripping the envelope tighter with the other. My mind is flooded with so many questions I can't think straight. So I start with the basics. "What?"

"Kory Summers. I've kept tabs on her since…" She shrugs and looks away. "You know."

"What the fuck, Pandora?" I say, standing up so fast my chair smacks into the window behind me. "You knew where she was this whole time?"

"Don't pretend like you didn't want me to know, Henry. Ignorance doesn't suit you." She looks at me with hard eyes but leans back in her chair calmly. "We all know you never got over her. Not even for a second did you ever let the flame you kept burning for her dim. So don't act like you're not about to explode on the inside at this information."

"But why would you do this? Why now? It's been ten years and you're just now telling me?" I pace back and forth as all the wheels in my head begin spinning at once.

I know exactly where her mom lives. I bought the building as soon as I got part of my trust fund. I kept the rent low enough that her mom would never leave or have to worry about making a payment. I ride by there at least once a week to check on things and speak to the property manager.

"Look, I could have told you a thousand different times before today," she says, leaning forward and putting her elbows on her knees. "But from what I saw, she was happy. She was living her life in Boston, and as much as I love you, it wasn't my place to step in."

"You're damn right!" I yell, and that takes Pandora by surprise. "It wasn't your place then and it isn't your place now. What good is going to come from you giving me this information? What am I supposed to do? Run to her mom's house and beg a woman I haven't seen in a decade to love me? Do you know what I've had to do to cope in a life without her? Do you have any idea the pain I've felt every single day that she wasn't with me? I found my soul mate when I was eighteen years old and had to let her go. This is going to rip me in two, Pandora."

She stands up from her seat and places her hands on my desk. "Henry, look at yourself. You never moved on. You had one day with her, and it changed you forever. You have to see this through. If you don't, you'll never heal, and you can't keep living like this." She straightens up. "I can see it in you as time goes on. Every year that passes, we lose more of you, and I know this is why. Open the goddamn envelope."

Those are her last words as she turns and walks out of my office, closing the door behind her. I grip the envelope so tight that it crinkles in my hand. I look down at it and release it, smoothing it as much as possible. I place it on my desk and fall down in my seat in front of it. I put my face in my hands and think over my options.

Then I realize I don't have any. I'll open the envelope, because there's no way I can't.

I reach for the letter opener and slice it down the paper in one quick swipe. Inside I find a few folded pages and I flatten them out on the desk. The first few pages detail where she went when she left our school.

Kory had tested out of her senior year early and was waiting to decide on what college she wanted to go to before she left. She received acceptance letters to five Ivy League schools, and she chose Harvard. She graduated early as a chemical engineer and went to work for one of the leading cosmetic companies in the country. She was there for several years before taking an abrupt job offer in Manhattan.

The next page is her personal history, and there Pandora has her listed as single, never married. The knot in my chest relaxes, and I'm surprised because I had no idea it was there. It wouldn't have mattered if she was married. That wouldn't stop me.

Wait, what am I thinking? Am I really doing this? Do I have a choice?

The rest of the pages are filled with information about where she lived and what she was up to in Boston. There's not much else that's known about her situation in Manhattan, other than the fact that she's living with her mom in the building I own, and she's got a job that's about a block from me.

I stand up and start pacing. I could walk over there right now and wait to pretend to bump into her. I could walk into the building and just ask for her. It's not like she doesn't know who I am.

Then I think back to the last time I saw her, and the tears in her eyes. However much time has passed, that's still the image that's burned into my brain. I can't think of a single reason why she would want to see me. But that was then, and I never got a chance to explain myself. She never stopped to let me tell her the truth, and it's time for me to change that. In fact, it's pretty fucking long overdue.

I'm pacing with purpose now because a plan is forming. The only logical thing to do now is to make it so she can't run. This time she's going to hear me out. This time I won't let her get away.

Chapter Three

Kory

I finish putting on my lipstick, happy with the way everything seems to be falling into place this morning. I feel like it's the first good hair day I've had in forever, and it helps that my lip is no longer bruised and puffy. I was thankful it had gone away before my mom got back from vacation. I'm even more thankful that I hadn't heard a word from Jason.

Maybe he's letting it go. I've been debating reaching out to his wife. I don't know how to handle that. I don't want to be back on Jason's radar, but I also think she needs to know about the man she's married to. Doesn't she deserve it? She lies in bed next to him every night, and the thought makes my stomach turn.

Putting the lid on my lipstick I put it into my purse then exit my bathroom. I make my way to the kitchen and smile when I see my mom up and making breakfast.

She's been over the moon about me being back home, which has made me a little slower on finding a new place to live. She turns around when she hears me, and a giant smile brightens her face. Her curly gray hair bounces a little, and it makes me realize how happy I am to be home.

"I made chocolate chip pancakes," she sing-songs, making my heart ache a little more. It's always just been her and me, making us superclose.

My mom wanted a child more than anything in the world, so she chose to go through artificial insemination. I never had a dad, but I never felt like I was missing out either. My mom filled this house with so much love that there was never room for me to wish for something else.

"Bacon?" I tease.

"Always," she says, setting a plate in front of me at the breakfast bar. "How goes the new job?"

"Good. I really love it. I have more freedom, and they give me free rein with all my ideas. It's refreshing," I tell her.

Being back in New York has been better than I thought it could be. I feel more like myself. I don't know why I've been running from it for so long. This might not have been my plan, but it's turned out to be a fantastic opportunity. I'm putting my past behind me and not shedding any more tears. It's also hard to be sad when I'm getting to spend more time with my mom.

"That's good, honey." My mom kisses me on the top of the head. "I'm supposed to meet Susan this morning. Have a good day at work," she says, picking up her purse and heading for the door. Sometimes I wonder how we're related. My mom can't seem to sit still while

I'm content on the sofa with a book for days. That said, I love that she's so active.

I dig into my breakfast, feeling better than I have in weeks. My reasons for hiding from New York all this time seem so small and stupid now. I've felt more content since I've been here, but a mom can do that to you. Maybe all I really needed was to be around her again.

After putting my plate into the dishwasher, I grab my purse and laptop bag and jet out the door. I make it down the stairs and then freeze when I see it's pouring rain outside. Great.

Not wanting to make the walk to the subway, I have the doorman wave me down a cab. He motions to me a second later, and I run out, jumping in as quick as possible, yet still getting a little wet. The door shuts and I pull out my compact and see my mascara has run a little. Apparently the waterproof I'm testing isn't holding up so well. I'll need to add that to my list.

I lean my head back, letting my eyes fall closed for just a second. I stayed up way too late reading last night, and I know I'm going to feel it for the rest of the day. I wish I liked coffee like the rest of the world. It would be wonderful to have something wake me up on a day like this. Maybe I could try some hot cocoa for a sugar rush.

My eyes pop open when someone slides into the seat next to me.

"Hey, buddy, this one's taken!" the cab driver shouts.

I'm frozen as I focus on the man who's sitting next to me. I can't even find words. Time has gone by, but I'd never forget his eyes. They stare at me, and he seems to have the same reaction. My heart starts to pound. Silence falls between us for only a beat before he speaks.

"Take her where she needs to go, then drop me after." He reaches into his back pocket and pulls out his wallet. He hands the cab driver a stack of bills and the driver looks at them before pulling away from the curb.

I'm still shocked that I'm sitting next to Henry. Part of me wants to jump out of the cab. Another part of me wants to pretend that I don't care. That this is a happy accident and I've moved on.

Before I can react to him being in the cab with me, his mouth is on mine, taking me by surprise. His full lips press against mine as his hands go to my hair in a possessive hold. His tongue pushes into my mouth demanding entry, and my body obeys, giving him what he wants.

All the time that separated us falls away, and I melt. His mouth makes love to mine, and for a single moment I give in to what I've longed for, for over ten years.

But as all dreams do, this one comes to an end, and I realize what's happening. Reality falls around us, and I push against his chest, breaking our kiss, then smack him right across the face. I take myself by surprise at the action, but I don't apologize. I can't believe I really just did that.

The sting of the slap lingers on my palm, and damn it, Henry smiles at me, making me want to smack him again.

He's even more handsome than I remember, and I don't know if that makes me hate him more or less. My eyes begin to water as all the suppressed feelings I've had for him come rushing forward.

"Don't," I snap.

"God, I've missed seeing your face," he says, ignoring my words.

He reaches out, tucking a lock of hair behind my ear. I stare at him, still shocked to see him. How is this even possible? The one person in all of New York I wanted to avoid is sitting beside me in my taxi. The man I've dreamed about for years. The man who shattered my heart and made me never trust any man again. I'm a twenty-eight-year-old virgin thanks to him, and I want to scream at him, but instead I get lost in his eyes.

"I've missed you," he adds, and a tear slips down my face. I swipe it away as fast as I can, hating that I gave him that. I don't want him to know he has this effect on me.

To my shock, the taxi stops, and I see I'm at work. I jump out, hoping to get away, but he follows suit, chasing after me.

"Kory! You're not getting away from me again. I can promise you that," he yells from somewhere close behind me, but I move faster, pushing through the doors of my building. I scan my ID card to get through and hit the elevator button. He keeps calling my name, and panic rises in my chest. I push the button over and over like it will make the elevator come faster. I've got to get away from him.

Too many emotions are pushing forward and I just need distance. I feel like I can't breathe.

"Kory!" he barks again. I glance over my shoulder

to see a security guard pushing him back. The elevator doors finally open and I flee inside, pushing the button for my floor. When the doors close, relief floods me.

I can't believe what just happened. I fall back against the elevator wall. My pounding heart finally starts to calm as I reach my floor. I take a breath, trying to get myself together. I step off the elevator and head for my office, then drop off my bags at my desk before heading for the lab. I want to get lost in my work and not think about Henry Osbourne.

Henry.

The man I've dreamed about so many nights. The only man to ever turn my head. The only man to ever take my heart.

I try to forget about the incident, but my mind keeps going back to him. That kiss. How long have I wanted to know what it would feel like for his lips to meet mine? God, I'm ridiculous. How am I twenty-eight and just having my first kiss? It's pathetic. *What happened to being strong, Kory?* I scold myself. Maybe I've been lying to myself all this time. I bet he's had hundreds of kisses. The thought makes my stomach roll with nausea.

I hate the idea of him kissing other women. In school all the girls wanted him, and they complained about how he never dated. I think it's part of the reason why it drove them crazy that he asked me to the prom. Not only was he set to be one of the richest men in the world, but he ignored all the girls. Except me. It made me feel special, and for a short time, I let that feeling take hold.

I should've known it was too good to be true—the

most popular and most handsome boy in the school giving me attention.

A throat clears, making me look up from what I'm doing. Henry leans against the doorjamb, as casual as can be. As if he owns the place.

I stand up and my mouth falls open. I'm shocked at how he got in here. Everyone needs to be cleared and have a name badge. Or so I thought.

"What are you doing in here?" I demand.

"You're not running from me anymore," he replies easily. I glance around the room, wanting to flee, but there's nowhere to go. He takes a step into the lab.

I shouldn't be shocked he got in here easily. I bet with one call he was able to pass the security and was told where I was.

"Don't do this."

I hate how weak I sound. I thought I was past this, but something about Henry makes me unable to think straight. I want to tell him all my problems and have him comfort me. Which is crazy. It's been ten years. I don't even really know him, but just like years ago, he feels like home. Like he's mine.

"I'll buy this whole company if that's what it takes to get you to talk to me."

I stare at him, knowing he has the means to do this.

"What do you want?" I snap, my anger rising.

"You." His voice is deep and filled with certainty. It's like he's been waiting on me to ask the question, and the answer takes me by surprise. My heart flutters.

"You shouldn't be here." I pull my goggles off my face. I don't want to address what he just said.

"There isn't any other place I should be," he responds, closing even more distance between us. I step back, nearly tripping over my own feet, and remind myself how awkward I used to be as a teenager. He's bringing it all back.

"I want you to leave." I don't want all these emotions he's churning up inside me. He's bringing back everything I've fought to forget.

"Have dinner with me." His voice is like velvet.

"No," I reply instantly.

"I'm not leaving until you agree."

I study his face. He's changed over the years. The time when he still had a baby face is long gone; he looks like a man now. But there's something about him that remains the same, and the part of me that wanted it back then can see it.

Broad shoulders, hard facial features, and his blue eyes aren't as soft as they once were. It's easy to see he has power even without knowing him. He exudes control.

"Then take a seat." I motion to the chair in the corner of the room. Without missing a beat he walks over and sits down. I'm a little shocked but return to my work.

I wait for him to say something else, but he doesn't. I feel his eyes on me as I turn around and try to concentrate on my tasks.

Hours pass and he sits there watching me. He hasn't said another word and neither have I. The whole day has been wasted because his presence is making it impossible for me to focus. I've felt his stare on every inch of me, and it's more than I can handle.

I've had enough and I slam my hands on the table. "Fine!"

He stands up and walks over to me. "I'll pick you up at five when you leave work."

Before I know what's happening, he snakes an arm around my waist, pulls my body against his, and takes my mouth in a deep kiss.

I should fight him, but my body does the opposite of everything my head is telling it to do. It feels like my heart has found its missing piece, and I give in.

His palms press against my spine, pulling me as close as possible. When they slide up to the top of my ribs, I gasp and jerk back. The pain from the bruising shoots up my torso, and the shock of it takes me by surprise.

"Did I hurt you?" Concern shows in his face.

"No, sorry, it's just… I…"

"Tonight," he says, cutting me off and placing a soft kiss on my lips.

He takes a step back and then smiles at me before leaving the room. I'm left alone in the lab wondering what I've gotten myself into. I'm not sure my heart can take much more.

Chapter Four

Henry

Kory and I didn't have much time together, but the things that reminded me of her never left. I saved what I could from that night, and I cherished it. Even if most of it was only a memory.

Seeing her today in the cab was more than I had ever imagined. I watched her run from her building into a cab, and I didn't have a choice. I jumped in the back without thinking, and then I mauled her like an animal. Maybe that's what I've become. I've been denied what I've wanted for far too long and I could only react to her presence. One look at her and I had to kiss her. All those years of fantasizing what it would have been like, and my imagination wasn't even close. The feel of her lips against mine, the curve of her body, and the sound she made when I tasted her.

I wasn't prepared for what seeing her would do to me, and I lost control. I almost lost it again when she got away from me in the building, but one phone call got me into her lab.

Watching her work for hours was strangely calming. It was as if my soul knew she was close and it could finally relax. We weren't going anywhere without her, and I made sure of it. I couldn't take my eyes off her as she moved around the room. From the way she held her hands to the way her legs crossed, she was erotic. Everything about her turned me on, and I didn't want to blink and miss something. It had been so long since I'd seen her, I didn't want to leave her side again. But this pit stop was important, and I want tonight to be perfect.

We've got some catching up to do, and I want all the cards on the table. I let her get away once, and I won't let it happen again. After all this time, I worried she might not feel the same way as I do. But after feeling her in my arms, and knowing she felt it, too, it's clear that not one thing has changed.

Chapter Five

Kory

When the clock strikes exactly five o'clock, I grab my bag and stand from my desk. Terror grips my throat, and I don't know if it's because I'm afraid Henry won't show, or if I'm afraid that he will. Today was somewhat productive after he left. I spend the past few hours trying to sink myself into work and forget about the possibilities tonight might bring. I've always considered myself a strong woman, once I grew up a little. I'm someone who doesn't need others, but with Henry I'm weak. I try to give myself a pep talk as I take the elevator down, but I know the second my eyes lock on his I'm going to be a goner.

When I get to the lobby I don't see him and a sinking feeling hits my chest. Would he really stand me up after the big fuss he made this morning in the lab? Just as I'm about to walk outside, one of the security guards comes over and smiles at me.

"Ms. Summers, if you'll follow me, please." She

holds out her hand in the direction I should go, and I realize this must be the way to Henry.

I follow her through the lobby and around the south entrance of the building. It's not my usual way of entering for work, so I don't come out this way much. It's close to Central Park, but my mom's place is in the opposite direction. So even though it's a much more beautiful walk out this way, I never get to enjoy it.

When I step outside, the security guard nods to me and smiles, then goes back inside the building. It's a warm night out, but there's a breeze and the sun is beginning to set. I look around and see a large fountain straight ahead, and there's Henry standing in front of it.

I put my hand over my mouth to muffle my gasp when I see him surrounded by candles and flowers. It's then I notice the whole place is free of people, and it's just him and me in this gigantic space.

I walk over, and he comes to meet me halfway. The smile on his face is from ear to ear and it's infectious. A giggle forms in my throat and the hollow place in my chest warms. Suddenly I'm a teenager again and I'm head over heels for a man I don't even know. I always thought it was a silly schoolgirl crush, but even now, after all this time has passed, my light for him never dimmed.

He leans in and I think he's going to kiss me again, but instead he wraps his arms around me in a hug and just holds my body to his. God, his warmth wrapped around me makes me want to cry. How I've ached for this embrace.

He places a kiss on the top of my head then moves

his lips to my ear. "I think I may have gone a touch overboard."

I laugh and lean back to look up at him. "You think?"

Once again, I look over to his display of candles and flowers, and I'm awed by the gesture. I can't believe he did all this.

"Are we eating here?" I ask, as he takes my hand and leads me over to the fountain.

"I wanted a quiet place to talk," he says, and his words are heavy. I know what he wants to talk about, but I don't know that I'm ready to visit that subject just yet.

"Henry—" I try to step away from him but he stops my movement. I shouldn't even be here after what he did to me at prom, but I finally want to know why he did what he did all those years ago.

He shushes me softly. "You promised me dinner, and I'm holding you to it. Come with me."

He leads me to the edge of Central Park, where there's a dock with rows of small boats. A man is there to greet Henry, and he takes us over to one of the boats. They are big enough for a couple of people and the one he takes us to is set up with candles and a picnic basket. It's so over-the-top romantic, and the girly part of me is squealing with excitement.

Henry speaks to the man before stepping into the boat and then holds out his hand to help me board. I hesitate for only a second, and before I know what's happening, his hands come to my lower waist and he lifts me, placing me inside it with him.

I laugh and shake my head as I take a seat across from him, and he grips the oars. He begins rowing us out onto the lake, and I look around at the fairy lights lining the trees and twinkling across the water.

"You did all this?" I ask, feeling like Ariel in *The Little Mermaid*.

"I wanted to make sure you couldn't run from me." He shrugs and winks at me.

His chiseled jaw and day-old stubble make him look even sexier in the shadows. I should probably be angry he got me in the middle of a lake in order to talk to me, but I kind of like that he's willing to do this to keep me.

"I'm a great swimmer," I say, leaning back in my seat, trying to seem in control, like he doesn't have the upper hand here.

I watch as he stops rowing to remove his jacket and roll up his sleeves. When he reaches up to pull his tie loose, every female part of my body goes on high alert at the skin exposed on his body. Suddenly I'm just as hot as he is out here, and it's only getting warmer.

"Like what you see?" He wiggles his eyebrows playfully, and I roll my eyes.

"Have you gotten cocky in your old age?"

"No, just hoping you like the view."

"It's not so bad," I hedge, not wanting to stroke his ego. But then I immediately think of all the things on him I'd like to stroke.

Jesus, get it together, Summers. Focus. He broke your heart.

"I'll take what I can get," he says as we come to a spot under a canopy of trees that has lanterns hung all around it.

"Do you do this for all your dates?" I blurt out, unable to stop myself. "Never mind, don't answer that." My cover-up is terrible and I wish I could take the words back.

"I don't date." His words aren't teasing, but instead firm and true. "You're the only woman I'd do this for, Kory."

"You don't know me." It's the only defense I have, and I think maybe if I say it enough that I'll start to believe it. "You thought you knew me a long time ago, but people change."

He hooks the oars to the side of the boat and leans forward with his elbows on his knees. "You're right, people change." His agreement is a painful truth, but one I think we both need to hear.

I look away from him, because if I keep staring into those blue eyes of his, I won't be able to hold back the tears.

"Look at me, Kory." I take a breath and then turn back to him, unable to deny him what he wants. "I grew up and I became a man, but my feelings for you never changed. I may not be the same person I was when I was eighteen, but my heart is stuck in that library where you smiled at me for the first time."

"Henry," I whisper, feeling a lump form in my throat.

"Just listen, baby," he says, getting on his knees in front of me. "I've spent the past ten years trying to convince myself that what we had wasn't real. Tried to deny the fact that the first time I held your hand I knew I didn't want to hold another for the rest of my life. That when I had you in my arms on the dance floor, I never wanted to dance with anyone else but you. We had one day together and it changed everything I knew to be true. I made myself believe that you didn't feel the same way, and that's how I made it through."

He reaches forward and takes my hands in his. His hands surround my fingers, and he brings them up to his mouth, grazing his lips across my knuckles.

"Three thousand seven hundred and twelve," he whispers, then stares into my eyes. "That's how many days I had to tell myself that it wasn't real. And then today, I kissed you, and I knew it was all a lie."

A tear slips down my cheek. I've done the same thing he has, trying to make myself believe something that every part of my soul fought against. But I gave my heart to him once, and the second he had it, he ripped it in two. I can't go through that again.

I pull my hands from his grasp and place them in my lap.

"Do you know what's gotten me through all these years?" I ask, straightening my spine. "Every time I thought about giving in and picking up one of your calls, I remembered what you did to me. Even years later, when a moment of weakness would make its way in, I would conjure up the image of you in that bathroom with your pants around your ankles and Cassie Springer naked and on her knees in front of you sucking your cock. Then I'd remember the sounds of everyone laughing at me and how stupid I was to trust you. That's what got me through it, Henry."

Chapter Six

Henry

Prom...

Tonight was perfect. Kory and I went to have our pictures taken with my family, and my parents loved her, just like I knew they would. Afterward we went to dinner with everyone and we laughed the whole time. I held her hand under the table and kept seeing her blush anytime I would look at her. God, she's so beautiful.

We danced until she said her feet hurt and then we sat in the corner of the ballroom and talked for most of the night. I'd never felt happier in my life just being with someone. It was crazy. It was like we were instant best friends, but there was something more. Standing near her somehow calms something inside me, and I don't want it to stop.

After they shut the ballroom down, some of the guys from my soccer team were headed to a lake house for an after-party. I wasn't sure I wanted to go, but when I asked Kory she said she wanted to. I felt like maybe she was saying yes because that's what she thought I wanted to do, but I didn't push it. I was driving and I hadn't been drinking, so we could leave anytime she wanted.

We got to the house about an hour ago, and we've just been hanging out on the porch talking since then. It's nice to be alone, not having to shout over the music.

"I told you I was a terrible dancer," *I tease as Kory slips off her heels and rubs her feet.* "Here, put them in my lap."

She laughs but props her feet up on my thighs, and I begin rubbing them.

"It's not you, it's me," *she says, and I tickle her foot in retaliation.* "Seriously. I'm such a klutz. I never walk in heels, and tonight wasn't the time to start. I didn't realize you were going to have me on the dance floor all night."

"What can I say? I found a beat and I shook my tail feathers." *God, how are my lame jokes actually making her laugh?*

"I like your tail feathers," *she says, and a moment of silence passes between us.*

Just when I'm about to say something, Marcus, one of my soccer teammates, comes out on the porch with a few of the guys behind him.

"Oh, captain, my captain, it's your turn for a shot," *he says, holding out the shot glass.*

"No can do. I'm driving tonight." *I feel Kory try to pull her feet from my lap, and I hold on to them so she can't.*

"Don't worry, we've got a bus to take the ships back home once they're finished cleaning up," *Marcus says, and the guys behind him start laughing.*

"What did you say?" I ask, my tone low and filled with anger.

"My bad, Henry," Marcus says, holding his hands up and taking a step back. "I thought this was a charity thing. No harm no foul."

The other guys fall around laughing and I'm pissed as hell. I stand up so fast the soda that was on the arm of my chair falls in my lap and spills all over my tux and Kory's feet.

"Shit, I'm sorry, Kory," I say, trying to wipe it off.

Her feet are out of my grip and we're both standing up before I notice everyone that was on the porch disappeared.

"Assholes," I grumble. "I—"

"Don't worry about it. Why don't you get cleaned up? I think I'm ready to leave," she says, and I can see some of the light in her eyes has dimmed.

"Okay," I concede, not wanting to ruin any more of our night. Coming here was a mistake and I shouldn't have done it. These people suck, and Kory deserves better. "Wait here. I'll be back in a second."

I open the sliding glass door and hear loud music coming from inside. I go into the house and find a few people in the kitchen, and I walk by without saying a word. I make my way through the living room, and there are some people in there doing shit I don't want to see, so I hurry to the back of the house, where there's a bedroom. I find a bathroom attached, so I close the door behind me and unzip my pants to take a piss before we get on the road. It's about an hour drive back and I don't want to have to waste any time stopping when I could spend it talking to Kory.

I grab some tissue from off the roll and try to blot off as much of the soda as I can, but it's no use. It's all wet. When I'm finished, I walk over to the sink, leaving my pants undone so I can try to wash some of the sticky syrup off my belt buckle.

I hear a slight knock and turn to the door. "Occupied!" I shout over the music thumping all the way in the back of the house.

When I hear the door open, I turn around to tell whoever it is to get out, but it's not who I expect. Cassie Springer, captain of the volleyball team, walks in and closes the door behind her.

"Cassie, what are you doing? I'm in here. Go find somewhere else."

She made it clear to me at the beginning of the year she'd do anything I wanted if I'd take her to prom. And then she proceeded to detail what that included via text. I finally had to block her number after she didn't like me turning her down. I'd heard she was pissed as hell when she found out I was taking Kory to prom, but I didn't give it much thought.

"Hey, handsome," she says, taking a few steps toward me but swaying a bit. It's obvious she's had a lot to drink. "I just thought you might like to see what you're missing out on tonight."

I'm fumbling with my belt to close my pants up as she gets closer to me.

"Cassie, get the fuck out of here. If someone sees you—"

"It's okay. I don't mind if you don't. I told you I'd do anything, and I'm true to my word."

She reaches up to the halter tie around her neck, and with one flick, her silky dress falls off her body and to the floor. She's standing completely naked in front of me, and I back up so fast I hit the wall behind me and knock a picture off of it. The crash is loud, but it does nothing to stop her coming at me.

She takes another step and stumbles over her own feet in her drunken state, and I have to hold my hands out to keep her from landing on me.

It all happens so fast I'm not sure what order it happens in, but one second I'm clutching my pants and the next, Cassie is on the floor in front of me, and my pants are at my feet because I had to let them go. At that exact moment, the door flies open and Kory is standing there staring at me with the group of guys from the porch behind her laughing their asses off.

"Kory!" I shout, but it's too late. She's running and I can't untangle myself from Cassie and my pants around my feet.

The guys come into the bathroom and all stare down at Cassie, who's fully naked. I see a short dark-haired girl pushing her way through and feel relief. "Julie, get over here."

Cassie's friend Julie is thankfully sober enough to know this situation is bad and helps me get her covered up.

I pull up my pants and get them buckled and help carry Cassie out to the bed. I want to get to Kory, but I can't leave a girl passed out drunk with these guys just standing around watching.

"I'm going to call her parents," Julie says, pulling out her phone. "She's going to be so pissed at me, but I don't know what else to do."

I nod and look around the room until I spot Marcus.

"You!" I bellow. I lunge at him and tackle him to the ground. We wrestle for a few moments before I punch him and he passes out. Anger has flooded my veins and I don't have time to deal with this shit. I look around the room to see everyone has cleared out.

I look back and see Julie is talking on the phone. She's got this under control. I don't see anyone else in the house as I run through, shouting Kory's name. When I get back to the porch, her shoes are still in the same spot, so she couldn't have gone far.

But I was wrong.

I spend the entire night searching for her in the surrounding woods before calling the cops and reporting her missing. But it turned out she walked home, or hitched a ride, because all the cops would tell me was that she was home safe.

I spend hours and hours trying to get her to talk to me, to hear me out. She won't even speak to me. I went to her house and banged on her door until her mom called security and I was banned from the building.

It was all a stupid misunderstanding and I'm broken in two because she won't just hear me out. One conversation and this would all be cleared up, but then there had to be something more. If only I can get her to hear me out, then maybe I can get to the bottom of why she ran.

Chapter Seven

Henry

Present day...

"Do you really think I'd do that to you?" I ask, seeing the raw hurt in her eyes.

"I know what I saw," she answers stubbornly.

I search her face, and though she's angry, there is something else there. It's the same look in her eyes I saw that first time in the library. It's fear.

"You're afraid," I say, still unmoving.

"I am not." Her tone is defensive.

"That's what made it so easy for you to believe I'd do something so horrible to you." The truth being brought to light is a powerful thing, and I watch as she begins to realize her own lie. "Look in your heart, Kory. Look at me now. I've made some mistakes in my life and I did some dumb shit as a kid. But when it came to you, I would've ripped out my heart before I'd harm yours."

I reach out and take her hands in mine, and she lets me. Tears build in her eyes and she looks away. She follows the light on the water, and it's a few moments before she speaks.

"I've spent so long hating you, but now I don't know what to believe." She releases a breath and then looks down at our joined hands. "We were young, but you were bigger than life. You had all this money and power, and girls were just waiting to get in line around you. I kept asking myself the whole time I was with you, *why me?* So when I saw you in the bathroom it was like all my doubts were confirmed."

"Why didn't you just let me explain?" I ask. "You took off and I was terrified something happened to you. I called the cops, Kory."

"Sorry about that," she says, and a smile pulls at her lips. "They were pretty confused when they came by my place and I was there."

I want to laugh, too, because I want to put all this bullshit behind us. "I didn't hook up with Cassie Springer that night, or anyone else after you."

Her eyes snap up to mine, and I see confusion in her expression.

"I gave my heart away when I was eighteen years old, and I was waiting for her to come back to me.

"I love you, Kory. I've loved you from the first moment I saw you, and I never stopped." I sit up, taking her face in my hands, brushing her tears away with my thumb. "And I never will."

"Oh god, Henry, my heart can't take this." She leans forward, kissing me with so much passion. She pours it all into the space where our lips meet, and I know then that all the things that separated us have melted away.

I pull back to look at her. I don't want this dream to go up in smoke. "Is this real?" I ask, feeling myself smile.

"I love you, too," she says, her eyes shining. "I tried to make it stop, lied to myself that I had but I couldn't, and I didn't want it to."

I sit back abruptly and grab the oars.

"What are you doing?" There's a laugh in her voice now, and it's music to my ears.

"We're going home."

"I can't believe this is your place," Kory says as I pick her up and carry her into the house. I close the door behind us and spin her around, pinning her to it.

"I'll show you every square inch later. Right now, I need you." I kiss her with desperation and desire as I reach down and hike her thighs up around my waist.

My mouth moves down her jaw and to her neck, devouring her soft skin. Her moans and the sound of my name on her lips are like every fantasy I've ever had come to life. I grip her ass and grind against her as my lips find the warm place between her breasts.

"Don't stop." She knots her fingers in my hair as she rocks her hips. It's almost enough to have me coming undone before we've taken five steps in the door.

"Wasn't planning on it, baby," I say as I pull the top of her dress down, revealing her pink nipples. "Not ever."

I suck one tight bud into my mouth and feel her body shudder in my arms. I move to the other, needing to taste all of her.

"Holy shit, that's so good." Her words come out in gasps as she tries to catch her breath.

"Wait until I do it to your pussy." I move down to my knees and throw one of her legs over my shoulder. Pushing up her dress, I see her cream-colored panties are wet and I groan at the sight. "You've been put on this earth to kill me. I just know it."

I hear her soft giggle before I pull them to the side and cover her with my mouth. Her giggle turns into a cry of pleasure followed by a low moan as I slide my tongue through her wet lips. She tastes like cinnamon and spice and everything nice, and I want to live between her legs.

"Fuck, I've dreamed of this," I whisper against her wetness. "I don't know if I'll survive this."

"I won't survive if you stop!" she shouts, and grinds down on my mouth.

Her body reacting to mine as she searches out the release only I can give her makes me feel like a king. This is so much more than I ever hoped for, and I don't want to slow down to think about it now. I'm terrified if I blink that I'll wake up and none of this will be real.

Her legs tense and her thighs tremble. The grip she has on my hair tightens as her body coils with her imminent release. Being able to give her body this gift is what my fantasies are made of, and I flick my tongue across her clit in steady, even strokes to get her off.

"Henry!" she shouts, and the echo in the room makes me growl like an animal.

I want to mark every inch of her as mine and then do it all over again. I want my name to be the only one on her lips, and I want it now. I've waited a decade to have her under me and I won't wait any longer.

Her warm release hits my tongue and I drink it down. When she slowly comes down from her high, I kiss her pussy gently one last time then lower her leg to the ground. I stand up, then scoop her up in my arms, carrying her through the house.

"More," she mumbles against my neck, and she brushes her lips against the skin there.

"You can have as much as you want, baby." I hold her closer to me, squeezing her ass as I walk. "I'm all yours."

"I like the sound of that," she answers, then pulls back to look at me.

"Get used to it."

When I walk into the bedroom, there's a sliver of light coming from the bathroom and moonlight pours from the window. I want to turn on a spotlight and see every inch of her, but I also feel like this moment is special, and I don't want to scare Kory with my maddening desire for her. So instead, I let the soft glow surround her as I place her in the middle of the bed.

I climb on top of her and put some of my weight on her body as her arms and legs wrap around me. When I kiss her, the taste of her passion is passed between us and it spurs on my need. I don't know how much longer I can wait.

"I love you so much. Let me show you," I say, moving my lips down her neck.

"Henry, I've never done this before. I'm not on the pill or anything. I didn't expect this to happen when I woke up this morning." There's a slight hysteria in her voice, but as my mouth goes to her breasts, she relaxes again.

"I've never done this either, so we'll both just have to figure it out as we go. But I'm fairly certain after what just happened against my front door, we can make it work." I pull her dress down the rest of the way, sliding it off her body and leaving her in only a pair of panties. "And I'm not worried about protection. I've only ever wanted one woman in my life, and if the first time we made love, we made a baby, it would make me the happiest man alive."

"Is this another way to keep me from running?" she asks as I reach down and slip her panties off her hips.

"You're never going to run from me again, Kory. I'll make sure of that." I take off my shirt and slacks, leaving on my underwear as I lie on top of her naked body. "But I plan on putting a baby in you as soon as I can because I've waited long enough. We've got years of making up to do, and I'm not slowing down again."

She brings her hands to my waist and she pushes down my boxer briefs. She reaches inside and encircles my cock with sure fingers, rubbing it up and down.

"You keep that up and I'm going to get the sheets pregnant instead of you."

"Well, we can't have that," she whispers as she guides my cock to her opening.

The tip of my cock slips through her wetness, and I hiss at the sensations. It's warm and soft, and I want to push through her folds and sink every inch into her tight body.

She leans up to my ear as I put most of my weight on

her body and lean down on my elbows. I place a kiss on her neck as her lips go to my ear.

"I love you, Henry."

They're the words I've longed to hear since the day I met her, and I can't hold back anymore. I thrust into her all the way, feeling her tense for a moment as we both lose our virginity. She's the only home I've ever wanted and I finally have it wrapped around me.

I tell her of all my love, over and over as I place soft kisses on her. I try not to move as her body adjusts to the new sensation, and soon I am rewarded. She slowly rocks her hips under me, and as she relaxes, she becomes bolder.

I move with her, and though it's cliché, our bodies truly become one. I've never been more connected to a soul, and making love has wound us impossibly tighter to one another.

I stare into her eyes and hold her hands in mine. The moonlight shines on her face and I don't know how but she looks even more beautiful than she already is. My heart grows and so does our passion, and soon neither of us is content with the slow, steady pace.

Giving us what we both desperately need, I move my hips so that each thrust grazes across her clit. After only a few long strokes, she's ready to climax and I'm doing all I can to hold off until then.

When her body stops fighting it, she opens her legs and screams out my name as she peaks. I feel the pulses of her climax all along my shaft and I can only follow her over the edge. I see stars as the pleasure hits me, and it takes everything in me to keep from collapsing on top of her in a heap.

Instead, I cling to her, and when I feel her body become limp under me, I roll us over and wrap my arms and legs around her.

"I can't move, Henry. There's no way I could run." I feel her smile against my chest, but I don't let go.

"Just making sure you don't try to hit it and quit it." She laughs, and it runs all the way down my cock, which is still inside her. I thrust up, wanting to feel it again, and her laugh turns into a moan. "I'm not finished with you."

"I'll never leave you again," she vows, sitting up and looking down at me. "I'm home."

"Forever," I say, and she nods.

I hold her hips as she begins to move, and we make love all over again.

Chapter Eight

Kory

"Call out sick," Henry says as he trails kisses down my spine.

"I can't! I just started working there." Though I really wish I could. At this moment I never want to get out of this bed. I didn't know I could ever be this happy. I'm so pissed at myself for not hearing him out all those years ago. I could have spent the past ten years waking up to this.

"Maybe I'm your new boss."

I roll over to look up at him. His face is straight. No evidence that his words are a joke. "You didn't!" I snap. I want to be annoyed, but part of me loves that he'd do something like that.

"Don't like the idea of someone else bossing you around," he says, his dimples as bright as can be. Then they suddenly drop away. "What the fuck?"

His gaze drops to the bruise that still lingers on my ribs. All the playfulness we just had washes away. I don't want to think about Jason right now.

"I...ah—"

"Don't do that. You're about to lie." My eyes fall closed. "I want a name," he demands, and I open my eyes. How does he know? Maybe he can just read me well...

"Jason. He's my old boss." Henry is out of the bed before I can finish my sentence. His phone is at his ear, his expression murderous. "Henry, stop!" I lunge for him, but I'm not really sure what my goal is. I want Jason to pay for what he did but also want to move past it. He could do it to some other woman, but I also don't care for the idea of having to face him either.

Henry catches me easily, his phone falling to the floor. It's then I realize that I'm completely naked. "Fuck," Henry grunts, and I find myself back on the bed, pinned under him.

"Never in my life did I think I'd get a naked Kory chasing after me." He smiles at me before his mouth meets mine in a deep kiss. I melt into him before I remember I really need to get to work. I push on his chest and he lets my mouth go.

"Work," I moan.

He drops his forehead to mine. "My chair better still be in your lab, cause I'll be spending my day in it."

I giggle thinking he's joking, but when I really look at his face I know he's not.

"You think I'm letting you out of my sight until I got this Jason shit locked up?"

I lick my lips. Once again I know I should be annoyed, but that's not what flutters in my heart. I love that he's so protective of me.

"Your chair will always be there," I tell him. I'll never push him from my life again. If he wants to follow me around everywhere, I'll let him. "But we need to get moving. We still need to go to my place to get clothes."

"I don't run a billion-dollar company without knowing how to be prepared, baby," Henry says as he pulls me from the bed and tosses me over his shoulder. I squeak as he drops me on his sofa. I see tons of bags littering the floor. "I'll have your stuff moved over today."

"Henry." My eyes start to water.

"I'll work on your mom. I bet she probably hates me, but I'll spend the rest of my life making her like me. I'll do whatever it takes."

With that, the tears I'm holding leak down my face.

"Baby, don't cry." He kisses them, stopping them in their tracks.

"You say all the right things." I hiccup.

"Well, trust me, I know how mad your mom is at me. She spent many nights blocking me from you. She even smacked me a few times."

I gasp. It's hard to think of my mom smacking anyone.

"Trust me, babe. She has a good smack."

I rub my hand across the thin beard he has. "I like this," I tell him.

"Then I won't shave."

"There anything you wouldn't do for me?" I ask, smiling up at him, thoughts of Jason long gone.

"Give you up," he says instantly.

"I promise I'll never ask that again."

"Well, you better get ready or I'm never letting you out of here."

I debate calling in for a moment but know I'm going to have a lifetime with this man. It's clear after last night it's always going to be us.

I make myself stand up. Henry watches me as I shuffle through the bags. I can't believe how many there are; it looks like he cleared out a department store.

"You just going to watch me?" I tease, looking over my shoulder.

"Babe, you're fucking naked. Yeah, I'm just going to watch you."

I throw him a half-hearted eye roll, pulling out a blue dress and a pair of panties.

Henry narrows his eyes at the panties. "Fuck. I didn't think about panties. I sure don't like the idea of my male assistant picking out your underwear."

"I highly doubt he did. Probably had a personal shopper do it," I say as I slide them on. I should probably shower, but I like the idea of smelling like Henry all day.

"Still don't like it," he says, standing from the sofa as I pull the dress on over my head. Henry comes and places a kiss on my back before zipping it.

"Shall I take them off and go without?" I turn my head and bat my eyelashes at him.

"You're not walking around without underwear all day. I'll be thinking about bending you over every surface, and then I'll be thinking about someone getting a look at what's mine. I'll be horny and pissed all day."

I turn and wind my arms around his neck. "You're the only one who's ever seen it. No need to get jealous."

"Yeah, but I want to make sure it stays that way," he says before his mouth takes mine.

"We're never getting out of here," I laugh against his mouth.

He reluctantly lets me go. "Go finish getting ready," he tells me with a sigh. I dart off to the bathroom and do my morning routine. This all feels too good to be true. I look at myself in the mirror. I look well loved. I hate that I have to go to work. Normally I love working, but today it doesn't have the same attraction. Maybe it's because I used it to get lost in. Now I just want to get lost in Henry.

I walk back in to see Henry on his phone. "Make the calls," I hear him say before he turns around, sliding his phone into his pocket, and sees me. "You ready, baby?"

My heart flutters at his term of endearment. Even though he's used it before, it's still new. "Yeah."

He kisses me below my ear, then grabs my hand and leads me out.

When we get outside there is a car waiting for us. He motions for the driver to not open the door and instead opens it for me himself. I slide in and he follows suit.

"I need to see your mom today," he says, taking me a little by surprise. "I want to settle anything that could stand between us."

I look into his deep blue eyes. "Okay." I nod in agreement. I don't want anything between us either. I had no idea what had gone on between my mom and him until today.

The drive to work is all too quick. I hate getting out of the car and leaving him, but he follows me. I turn to look at him. "I wasn't joking," he says.

"You really bought the company?"

He shrugs like it's no big thing. "Not leaving you until this Jas—"

His words are cut off when someone yells my name. It's almost as if Henry conjured him. Jason is storming at me. I take a step back and almost lose my footing. Henry catches me before putting himself in front of me.

Fear takes hold of me for a moment, then Henry is on him. One solid punch and Jason hits the concrete. A few security guards I didn't notice before this flood in. Henry barks at them to step back as he takes a few more punches at Jason.

"How does it feel to have someone your own size come against you?" He hits him again. Blood pours from Jason's nose. "Guessing you don't fucking know." He slams his head into the ground, knocking him out.

"Sir," one of the security guards says, trying to calm him, but it looks like nothing will. My eyes meet the security guard's, and he motions to me to get him to stop.

"Henry." I say his name softly. He lets go of Jason and turns to look at me. "Please." He looks back at Jason, then to me.

"Get in the car, baby," he tells me.

"Are you getting in, too?"

"Yeah." I reach out and grab him to make sure he really is.

"Take care of it," he tells the security guard, who nods as Henry slides back into the car with me.

"Did I scare you?" he asks as I grab the handkerchief in his suit jacket to wipe off his knuckles.

"No," I admit easily. "You'd never scare me." I glance up at him, feeling a little shy. "It was kinda hot. You standing up for me. Not letting him near me." He grabs me, pulling me into his lap so I'm straddling him. "I just don't want you to get in trouble."

"I won't. The cops were already looking for him. And, well, the mayor owes me a few favors."

I shake my head. "Of course he does." I can't help but giggle.

"Not taking you back there today," he growls, pulling me closer.

"Hmm. Maybe I can work from home. There anything my new boss would like me to do?" I tease.

"I can think of a few things." I move against him, feeling his hard erection.

I try to slide off his lap, wanting to take him in my mouth.

"Baby," he growls. "We wait until we're home. No one sees you like this." I glance over my shoulder to see the driver and feel myself blush. I can't believe he made me forget where I am. Only he can do that to me.

"I love you," I tell him, dropping my forehead to his.

"When we get home I want you to chant that over and over while I'm inside of you."

"Sounds like this is going to be the best day of my life."

Chapter Nine

Henry

It's been two days, and I can't stand it anymore. I want her to be mine in every way. I don't care if we've only been back together for two days. This was ten years in the making. But we can't seem to stop making love so I can do what I need to.

"Where are you going? Come back to bed." Kory reaches for me, and I look back at the bed to see her naked body spread out on the silky sheets.

"Why do you have to make everything so difficult?" I say, going back to bed and crawling on top of her. "I'm trying to do something and you're tempting me to the point of insanity."

"If you're crazy, then I hope they put me in the same cell as you." She leans in and lowers her voice. "Because I think I might be feeling the exact same way."

"Do you have any idea how hard it is for me to get out of this bed while you're naked?"

"If I had to take a guess, I'd say pretty hard." She

snakes her hand down between us and wraps it around my length.

"You're a witch." I hiss as her hands stroke up and down, slowly milking my hard cock. "Don't stop."

The tip of my cock brushes against her wet lips, and I feel pearls of cum leak out of me. A shiver rolls down my spine and I have to hold back the urge to enter her.

"Just once more," she whispers as she runs her tongue along the shell of my ear.

With her one request, I'm forgetting all my plans again. I grab her wrists and pin them above her head as I thrust hard into her. Her legs wrap around me, and she moans with delight as I take her roughly.

"Just once? Is that all you want, baby?" I grit my teeth as the tight grip of her pussy surrounds me.

"No," she breathes, and it's music to my ears.

"This is forever, isn't it?"

She nods, but I squeeze her hands, wanting to hear the words.

"Forever, Henry."

I'll never get tired of her telling me she's mine. That she and I are in this for the long haul. I knew from the beginning that it would always be the two of us. We were destined for it, and there was never any stopping it. No matter how hard we tried to screw it up.

"Say it," I growl, needing to hear the words.

"I love you," she says instantly, and I grow bigger and harder inside her.

Nothing turns me on more than to hear her admission of love. It's the one thing I need to hear, but she doesn't seem to mind saying it.

Her body tightens as her orgasm slides through her and she peaks with a shout. Her shaking thighs are tired from all of our lovemaking today, but neither of us can bring ourselves to call for a break.

I may die in this bed between her thighs, but I don't think I could ask for a better way to go.

I'm unable to hold off any longer as the pulses of her pussy beg me to join her in paradise. I wrap my arms around her and grunt out my release inside of her. Our bodies are slick from passion, and it's primal and real. I've never been more open and honest with anyone in my life, and the intimacy we share is unlike anything I've ever experienced.

"Now can I get up from the bed?" I ask, rubbing my nose against hers.

She nods with her eyes closed. She's smiling, but she looks like she might fall asleep. When I pull out, she groans at the loss and I kiss her softly before I get up from the bed and go to the closet.

I reach for the box at the top, pulling it down and taking it back to the bedroom with me. Kory is on her side with her eyes closed, but when I sit down on the edge of the bed and watch her, she opens them sleepily.

I brush a lock of hair off her shoulder and lean over, kissing the bare skin there. "I've got a present for you."

Her smile grows as she looks at me then at the box in my lap. "What is it?"

Carefully, I open the lid and push away the white tissue. Kory sits up and looks down into the box as I pull out a pair of white shoes covered in rhinestones. They sparkle in the light and it takes her a second before she recognizes them. When she does, she gasps and puts her hand over her mouth.

They're the shoes she left on the porch the night of the prom. I look up to see surprise on her face, but I only smile at her. It was the only thing she left behind, and all I had to keep with me all these years.

"I see you remember them," I say, and she nods, still not saying a word. "I didn't bother letting every girl in town try them on, because I knew who my princess was, even back then. When I found them that night on the porch, I couldn't leave them. So, in my panic while looking for you, I brought them home with me." I look at the shoes and then back at Kory, smiling. "After I found out you were okay, I held on to them, thinking that maybe they'd be a good excuse to see you again. I kept telling myself that if I had them, then you'd have to see me."

"Henry, I'm so sorry. All those years wasted—"

I place a kiss on her lips, silencing her apology. We both made mistakes.

"After time passed and I knew you weren't going to speak to me, I realized I was keeping them for selfish reasons. That if I had one part of you, no matter how small, then it was real. We were real."

I place the box in her lap and take her hands in mine.

"I saved these, hoping that one day I'd get to place them on you again. I wished with all my heart that we would find our way back to one another. That I'd get to see you wearing them one more time in a white dress. I hoped—when there was no reason to—that you'd have these on while you were becoming my wife."

There are tears in her eyes, and I wipe them away.

"Become my wife, Kory. Finish what we started ten years ago and spend your life with me. Make me your husband and let me be a father to our babies."

"Yes," she cries as she throws herself at me.

She hits me so hard she knocks me back on the bed, but I wrap my arms around her and roll us over until I'm on top of her.

"Yes?" I ask, needing to hear it again.

"Yes! Yes! Yes!" she exclaims, laughing and kissing my lips.

"I'll never get tired of hearing that," I say, sitting up and pulling her from the bed.

"Where are we going?" There's surprise and shock in her voice.

"To get married. You think I'm going to give you a chance to get out of my grasp? Think again, baby."

"You're joking," she says disbelievingly as I scoop her up in my arms and carry her into the shower.

"When it comes to you getting away from me, I never joke."

"I guess marrying me is one way to make sure I stay."

I smack her ass as I walk her under the spray of the water, and her giggles echo off the tile.

"I love you," I say, kissing her lips as the water runs between us.

"I love you, too."

Epilogue

Henry

One year later

"What's wrong?" I ask, coming up behind Kory and wrapping my arms around her.

She's holding our sleeping daughter, Anne, and though Kory looks content, I know her better than anyone else in the world. I can see the fine line of worry on the back of her neck, and all is not well.

"I'm just nervous about leaving her."

I kiss her on the neck and rest my chin on her shoulder, looking down at our baby. "Do you think that my parents won't be able to handle her?"

"No, that's not it," Kory says, sighing.

She knows they're very capable and loving, but being a new mom has been an adjustment. There's always family around to help, and Kory is a fantastic mother; she just worries.

"You know we're only going to be gone for a few hours." I turn her in my arms so she's facing me.

"You're right. I want a date night out." She places Anne in her bassinet and we tiptoe out of the room while she's still asleep.

When we go to the living room, we say hi to my parents and leave them with a list of instructions about a mile long. But they practically shove us out of the door, saying they want us to go have a good time.

"Are you ready?" I ask Kory as we step onto the elevator.

"I am," she says, taking my hand in hers. "What do you have planned for us tonight?"

I put in my key and hit the button for the rooftop. Normally this is only used for maintenance, but I thought for a night, we could make an exception.

"Where are we going?" Her voice is filled with excitement and it's infectious.

"It's a surprise," I answer, bringing the back of her hand up to my lips.

When the service doors open, the entire space of the rooftop is revealed, along with a view of the city. There are lights strung all around and candles light the way.

"Oh my god, how did you do all of this?"

Gravel crunches under her feet, and I pick her up, carrying her over to the place I have set up. There's a table with linens and a picnic basket beside it. Champagne chilling and soft music playing.

"I know you've been worried about our first night away, so I thought this would make things easier."

"You really are the perfect man," she says, placing a kiss on my lips.

"I know, but feel free to keep reminding me."

A small love seat has been placed so that it looks out on the city. I sit down with Kory in my lap and reach to the table beside the couch to pour us some champagne.

"Do you know what today is?" I ask as I pass her a glass.

"I think it's Thursday, but I could be totally wrong," she says, then giggles and takes a sip.

"It's the day I asked you to prom." A look of surprise hits her face, and then she brings her hand to my cheek.

"How do you remember that?" She kisses me and shakes her head. "What if I would have said no? Can you imagine how different our lives would have been?"

"I would have never let that happen. And that's something I can't imagine. There's not a world where you and I aren't together. It's that simple." I kiss her again, and we both take a sip of our drinks.

"You've been so perfect through the pregnancy and since Anna was born. I know I've been a crazy new mom, but I don't know how I would have done any of it without you."

"You've given me more than I can ever repay. It's my job to take care of you." I set our glasses down and wrap my arms around her as we listen to the music and watch the city below.

We kiss and cuddle as I feed her dinner while she stays in my lap. It's the perfect night and I know exactly what she needed.

"How do you do it?" she asks, and raises an eyebrow in question. "How do you know exactly what I want without me saying it, and give me the perfect night that I didn't know was possible?"

"You forget, there isn't an inch of your heart I don't know," I say, dipping her down on the couch and kneeling in front of her. I spread her legs and push the edge of her dress above her hips. "And there isn't an inch on your body I haven't had."

When my hands trail up her thighs, I see the hungry look in her eyes.

"Now sit back and let me enjoy the view," I say, kissing my way to the warm center between her legs.

Four years later

"What the fuck is that?"

I turn to see Henry standing a few feet behind me.

"What?" I look around to see what he's talking about. He takes off his suit jacket and drops it over my shoulders, making his cousin Pandora snort.

"What you're wearing," he bites out. I look down at my sports bra and yoga pants. This is the first time I've been okay with showing off my belly since I had our last baby, but I'm still trying to get in even better shape. Swimsuit season is around the corner.

"Workout clothes." I look at him like he's crazy because, well, he is.

"Anyone left in the room in the next thirty seconds will no longer have a job!" he shouts. We're in the company gym. Pandora had offered to help me with my workout routine. That didn't seem to be going so well.

The men that were in the gym practically run out. Pandora just shakes her head. "And I know that look cause my own hubs gets it. See you later." She picks up her water bottle. "Text me. We can work out at my house if need be."

"You're a crazy person," I snap at Henry.

"You're going to end up with a third kid in your belly."

I jump back. "You keep that thing away from me," I joke, good humor replacing my annoyance. I do want another baby. Growing up I thought school and a drive for work were what I wanted in life. I was wrong. I love being a mom and a wife more than anything in the world.

Henry can put as many babies in me as he wants.

"Miss your curves," he says, placing a hand on my hip. The suit jacket he'd put on me falls to the floor.

"That why you keep suggesting pasta for dinner every night?" A smile spreads on his face. I don't know why I've even been doing this working out crap. I hate it, but in the back of my head I thought maybe Henry would like it. Seems I was wrong.

He lifts me and walks me to the far wall, my back hitting the cool surface. I wrap my legs around him. I love when he goes all caveman. Even if I pretend to him I don't. His mouth takes mine in a deep kiss that's over before I want. "My office. There aren't any cameras there."

"We aren't having sex in your office," I tell him, knowing it's a lie.

"We always have sex in my office."

"Fine, but you're so not carrying me there," I fight back, knowing that's what he plans to do. "Unless you want me to go like this..." I motion to my workout clothes.

He mumbles some curses before putting me on my

feet and pulling out his phone. "Clear my floor. No one on it." I shake my head as he barks into his phone, then I'm thrown over his shoulder as he goes over to the elevator, swiping his key card so it will go straight to his floor.

"Caveman," I mutter, smiling.

"You love it," he throws back.

He's right. I love everything about him.

Epilogue

Henry

Nine years later

"Are you sure your parents are okay keeping the kids?" Kory asks as she walks through the kitchen.

Immediately I forget what she says because I'm too busy looking at what she's got on. It's a deep blue wrap dress that's halfway up her thigh and showing off way too much of her tits. It hugs her small waist and round hips, and her ass bounces with every step. She's got a body that tempts me every second of the day. And she damn well knows it.

My cock is hard and throbbing at just the sight of her. When the fuck did she get that dress? I want to go over to where she's standing and bend her over the nearest surface so I can fuck her while she's wearing it. But I want to look at her for a few more moments before I do it.

"Henry?" she says, and I blink a few times. "Are you okay?"

"No," I say, gripping the edge of the seat.

"What's wrong? Are your parents not able to keep the kids? I know they can be a little much, but Mallory and Miles begged to have them for the whole weekend, so I assumed—"

"Where did you get that?" I ask.

"My dress? You like it? I got it on sale at—"

"And you plan on wearing that out of this house?" I grit out, cutting her off again.

She narrows her eyes at me and puts her hands on her hips. "Is there a problem with what I've got on? Because I thought I looked pretty fucking hot in it."

"That right there," I say, standing up from the chair. "That's the problem. You do look pretty fucking hot in it."

A smile pulls at her lips and her hands drop from her hips. She turns to the side a bit, preening in her new dress and showing me every angle.

"You think so?" She bats her eyelashes at me, and it's a mistake. She's teasing a tiger right now.

Slowly I walk toward her and she sees my intention. She takes a step back for every one I gain, and the chase is on.

"Where do you think you're going?" I ask as she backs up against the island.

"Henry, I know that look. We don't have time." She looks around the room as if something can help me see reason. All I see is her in that dress. She's begging to be fucked.

"There's one thing I want to eat, and we don't even have to leave the house for it." I watch as her thighs clench together. "Are you wearing panties?"

The flush of her cheeks gives me my answer, and I take another step to put me right in front of her. The island is at her back and there's no place for her to go. I grip her hips and lift her, putting her ass on the edge and getting between her thighs.

"Spread them for me," I say without taking my eyes off hers.

I feel her thighs move on either side of me, and I glance down to see her short dress has risen up to her pussy.

"Is that all for me?" I lick my lips and wait until she nods. "That's what I thought."

I scoot her ass even more toward the edge as I kneel down in front of her and cover her with my mouth. Her flavor that I love so much hits my tongue and her fingers go to my hair. I reach down to my slacks and pull my cock out while I eat her, rubbing the length and pretending it's her pussy wrapped around it.

I jerk off while I lick her pussy just how she likes it. Her body has only gotten better with age. She teases me and says one day I'm going to be old and we won't be able to make love anymore, so we've got to get it all in now. It doesn't matter to me, though. As long as she still lets me hold her at night, I don't care.

"Henry, I need more."

I look up at her, and we lock eyes while my mouth is still on her pussy. I see the intensity there, and I know she wants me inside her. I've never been able to deny her what she wants, so I get to my feet and slide her slickness down on my shaft, filling her to the brim.

"That's it," I soothe as she clenches around me and clings to my shirt.

I grip her ass hard and lift her off the island as I stand there in the middle of the kitchen and bounce her up and down on my cock. Her wet pussy coats me, and I glide in and out, hitting her sweet spot in just the right rhythm.

She can't hold back and I feel her release run through her body as she holds on to me impossibly tighter. I grunt out my own inside her, swelling to the point of pain as her tight pussy squeezes me.

When I've given her all that I can, she's limp in my arms. I carry her over to the sofa while I'm still inside her and sit down with her straddling my lap. I hold her like that for a long time, just rubbing her back and kissing her neck. She's my whole world, and though these moments alone aren't as frequent as they used to be, they are just as beautiful.

"I'm not wearing this dress to dinner," she says, and I kiss the top of her head.

"Because it's covered in cum now?" I ask, and she looks up at me smiling.

"You're lucky I love you." She kisses me softly on the lips.

"Not a day goes by when I don't know that, baby." I kiss her again and then tuck her hair behind her ear. "Want to order in and eat in bed?"

Her eyes light up and she's already nodding before I can finish my sentence.

"Go get out of this dress and get under the covers. I'll grab the menus."

She leans down, kissing me one last time. This one is deeper than the last, and it's filled with all that we've built. It's love and respect, devotion and passion all rolled into one. It's our past and our future and everything in between. It's our story, and I love every part of it.

* * * * *

Acknowledgments

Thank you to Carina Press and the team of people that helped make this book happen. We loved this series so much and are thrilled that Henry got his story, too! Shout out to our editor, Angela James, for keeping us on track and finding the patience to work with us on yet another book... Oysters are overdue!

To our ride-or-die friends, thanks for feeding us too many carbs and sending panda gifs when we needed it the most. To our husbands, who always know exactly what to say and when to say it, you guys are the best.

Lastly, and most important, to our readers. There is an endless list of people who message us, send Snapchats, Instagram our books, and Tweet at us. We can't say enough what each of those shout-outs mean to us. We are forever grateful that you've come on this journey and paved the way for us to write the books you love. One day we're going to find a way to give back all the generosity and kindness you've show us, but until then, WE LOVE YOU!!!

About the Author

Alexa Riley is a pseudonym for the sassy dynamic duo of Melissa King and Lea Robinson. Both are married moms of two who love football, doughnuts and obsessed heroes in novels. They bonded over their love of steamy reads in the summer of 2013 and haven't been able to stop talking since.

Alexa Riley specializes in insta-love, over-the-top sweet and cheesy love stories that don't take all year to read. If you want something safe, short and always with a happily-ever-after, then these are your girls. As a team, they are *New York Times* and *USA TODAY* bestselling authors of more than thirty books.

Connect with Alexa Riley!
AlexaRiley.com
Facebook.com/AlexaRileyAR
Twitter.com/_AlexaRiley
Instagram.com/AuthorAlexaRiley